'Why did you let me do that?'

It was hard to utter a word. 'What?' Sophie asked stupidly.

'I thought you were engaged to Rupert.'

So that was what it had been about. What a fool she had been—a complete and utter fool! Deliberately Alex had exploited that powerful latent attraction to satisfy his own curiosity. And he must now know, too, just how devastatingly attracted she was to him.

Dear Reader

With the worst of winter now over, are your thoughts
turning to your summer holiday? But for those months in
between, why not let Mills & Boon transport you to
another world? This month, there's so much to choose
from—bask in the magic of Mauritius or perhaps you'd
prefer Paris...an ideal city for lovers! Alternatively,
maybe you'd enjoy a seductive Spanish hero—featured in
one of our latest Euromances and sure to set every heart
pounding just that little bit faster!

The Editor

Lucy Keane first started writing when she was six, got a
degree in English at Oxford, and subsequently pursued a
colourful career that ranged from working in the
wheeling and dealing world of the City to teaching
nursery rhymes to four-year-olds in New Delhi.
Innumerable hobbies include drinking chocolate in ski
huts in the French Alps and digging up Roman drains on
archaeological sites. She is an obsessional traveller, and a
dedicated researcher into real-life romance...

Recent titles by the same author:

RELUCTANT ENCHANTRESS

DANCE TO THE DEVIL'S TUNE

BY
LUCY KEANE

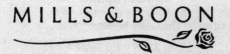

MILLS & BOON

MILLS & BOON LIMITED
ETON HOUSE, 18-24 PARADISE ROAD
RICHMOND, SURREY TW9 1SR

For Nicholas

*First published in Great Britain 1994
by Mills & Boon Limited*

© Lucy Keane 1994

*Australian copyright 1994
Philippine copyright 1994
This edition 1994*

ISBN 0 263 78492 4

*Set in Times Roman 10 on 11 pt.
01-9405-58857 C*

Made and printed in Great Britain

CHAPTER ONE

WELL, what *did* you do stuck in London in a hot August without a place of your own to move into for two months, and with no prospect of work? Sophie, bending uncomfortably at the knees, squinted at her image in the side-window of a big white car that almost lay in the gutter. Long blonde tendrils framed her face untidily, and she looked pinkish and out of breath. She tried, at the same time, to rearrange her hair with her fingers and justify what she now regarded as a most unwise decision.

In the past she'd had trouble organising herself and making up her mind about things, but not any more: the new Sophie was dynamic and decisive, and would therefore become brilliantly successful. At least, that was what one hundred and twenty one pages of *The Successful Businesswoman* guaranteed for all readers who followed its advice. But it was a pity that rather too frequently the new Sophie had found herself having to review her decisions in the light of vital factors she should have considered earlier—like the fact she wasn't good at reading music, in the present instance... Supposing she messed up the whole recording?

Never mind, she told herself firmly; all that was really needed was a bit of initiative! She leaned further forward to examine her eye make-up, and overbalanced. Instinctively she clutched at the car door-handle to steady herself—and the whole elegant London square was suddenly echoing with the screeching *eee-owww* of an anti-theft device. A pigeon tumbled out of the plane tree leaves with a squawk of shock.

She stepped back guiltily and looked round. There was no one else in the square. She rejected the idea of leaving a note on the windscreen: 'I did this', signed Sophie Carter, and fled instead for the sanctuary of the building she had been told was the recording studio. She had to take that on trust—it looked to her exactly like a church.

The main entrance was open, but a uniformed security guard stood just inside, barring the way to a set of double doors. He looked at her suspiciously—the burglar alarm was only too audible—and glanced up at the red light above the door. His manner was dismissive. 'The session's started,' he said shortly. 'You'll have to wait.'

It was true—great waves of piano music were breaking against the doors inside. Her friend Rupert must have had to begin without her.

She groped in her handbag and extracted a crumpled piece of paper—the recording schedule Rupert had given her, and her sole means of identification. There was a list of people to whom copies had been sent printed at the bottom: Alex Tarrant—she'd heard that name somewhere before—Derek somebody... Joe somebody... Her eyes didn't even take in the words properly. *Rupert Stretton*.

'Look!' she insisted. 'Here, this one's the pianist— I'm his page turner. I got held up on the Underground. I have to be in there!'

This time, the guard pursed his lips and eyed her doubtfully. 'Well, I dunno...' he said slowly.

But the new Sophie, detecting a weakness, didn't delay to debate further. Action was what was wanted! With an impatient flick of her blonde hair over one shoulder, she launched herself against one of the double doors energetically. The unexpected momentum carried her into the hall and she almost fell inside.

The recording studio looked like a nineteenth-century hall full of sunlight, but its high and ornate plasterwork ceiling, and immense windows glassed with plain squares, gave her the impression that she really had just stumbled into one of London's old churches by mistake. Then, across a vast sea of polished floor, she caught sight of her friend Rupert, islanded out in the midst of all that space at a grand piano.

The music broke off abruptly.

'In the nick of time!' he greeted her cheerfully. 'I've had to start with the only thing I can play from memory. It lasts about ten seconds.' As a sort of aside, without looking at the keys he began a trite little tune reminiscent of 'Chopsticks'.

Rupert was twenty-one, three years younger than Sophie, and had he been older she might have been susceptible to his obvious charms. He looked like everyone's idea of a very youthful and romantic concert pianist. His dark hair flopped artistically over a broad, intelligent forehead, and his blue eyes could definitely be described as 'soulful' when he gazed out into space over the piano. His classic features could have been those of some Greek god, but the age-gap, from her point of view, definitely put her in the category of big sister, despite the fact that he occasionally showed an inclination to flirt with her. And since his sense of humour verged on the practical joke, it would have been difficult to take him at all seriously, except on the subject of music. She wouldn't put it past him to have half sawed off the leg of the chair she was to sit on, in the hopes of a comic incident during the recording.

She liked him, but they hadn't been acquainted long and she knew very little about his personal life. He was good-natured and his sense of humour amused her, although she suspected his schoolboy crush on her could prove inconvenient if too much encouraged.

'I just can't resist leggy blondes,' he'd told her on their very first meeting at a friend's supper party, 'especially when they've got such melting brown eyes! Did you know that yours are a true almond shape?' But Sophie was hardly the ideal recipient of flattering remarks, however sincerely meant—her sense of the ridiculous rarely let one pass without comment. In this case, 'melting' made her eyes sound like nut chocolates that had been left in the sun. She'd lost no time in pointing it out.

Rupert had changed tack adroitly. 'Warmth,' he agreed. 'That's exactly what I meant! You've got eyes that are full of eastern promise—very mysterious and sexy. It's that sideways look you have sometimes. You'd better be careful—it's the sort of thing that's going to get you into trouble one of these days!'

'Is that a threat or a promise?' And she'd let her eyes slide sideways in exactly the look he had warned her about, just to tease him. But it had never occurred to her before that it was either mysterious or sexy; an old school friend had told her she merely looked calculating, and, as someone who had never seemed to calculate enough in life, she'd taken that as a *real* compliment.

Now Rupert gestured to her. 'Come and sit over here, on my left, but a bit back from the piano. I don't want to knock you off your perch in my more energetic moments. You look nice, Sophe. Much more glamorous than the average page turner. Why not sit a bit closer after all so I can have a better view of your knees?'

She hated that particular version of her name, and he knew it. 'Don't call me Sophe!'

Her high heels announced her progress over the wooden floor rather too loudly as she crossed to the centre of the hall, and she became conscious that somewhere outside the tell-tale *eee-oww* was still wailing unpleasantly. She tried to ignore it. Faced with the immediate prospect of working for her money, she was convinced it was not going to be as simple a matter as Rupert had made out.

He was surrounded by microphones, perched on their stands like weird birds in a forest of spindly trees. Behind him rose a wide-tiered platform, and at the opposite end of the room were double doors, flanked by staircases leading to an organ gallery, beneath which were a lot of oddly shaped packing cases stamped with the name of a famous orchestra.

She and Rupert appeared to be entirely alone.

'Isn't there anyone else here—I mean recording engineers or anything?' she asked, puzzled by their apparent isolation. 'And where's the control room? I thought they were supposed to have windows so they could see what's going on.'

Her ideas of a recording studio were hazy, based on what she'd seen on films.

Rupert started to explain, 'This used to be a church, but Alex bought it because it's got brilliant acoustics for classical mus——'

There was an electric crackle from a small speaker in the confusion of microphones, and a deep voice that would have been attractive if it hadn't sounded so irritated cut in, 'A little less of the chat, Rupert!' And then demanded, 'What was that crashing around just now?'

Rupert addressed his reply to thin air. 'My page turner's arrived.' He glanced at Sophie. 'Take your shoes off,' he advised, in a stage whisper, and then proclaimed loudly in the direction of the mikes, 'Even the walls have ears here—isn't that right, Alex?'

There was another crackle and buzz as of angry insects, and the disembodied voice, with a more perceptible edge of impatience this time, said, 'What the hell is that racket outside?'

There was an indistinct mumble in the background, and then the voice a little more distantly in curt reply, 'Get on, then, Joe, will you? Take the keys—and keep an eye open for anyone hanging around!' Then again more distinctly, 'Rupert? There's a lot to do this morning—we can't afford interruptions. You'd better inform your "page turner" that red lights indicate, "Recording in session: strictly NO entry".'

Sophie winced at the tone, steely with sarcasm. Thank goodness he didn't know it was she who had set off the car alarm! Joe, whoever he was, must have been sent out to deal with the siren, which meant that that long, low white machine crouching by the pavement in its multi-thousand-pound splendour belonged to the man with the sarcastic voice.

Overwhelmed by a burning impulse to justify herself to her unseen critic, she addressed the thicket of microphones. 'I thought Rupert wouldn't be able to start without me—sorry I'm late, but I couldn't get here any quicker!' Unintentionally, she managed to sound more aggrieved than apologetic.

'Couldn't you.'

It wasn't a question. It conveyed a complete lack of interest in anything Sophie Carter might have to say about herself, her life, existence in general, or the entire universe—and also the invalidity of any excuse she might have to offer, and the unquestionable superiority of the speaker—in precisely two words.

For all of six seconds she struggled with a feeling she could only identify as a sort of outraged surprise, then unwisely hissed at Rupert, 'Who *is* Alex?'

He replied at normal volume. 'Who—Alex? Oh, don't take any notice of him! He's just the bloke in charge— he happens to be producing the record.'

Oh. So that was why the name was familiar! She should have made the connection before. Alex Tarrant, thirty-one and mega-successful, and about to negotiate a much publicised deal with one of the big German recording companies, or so she'd read in the papers. Serious mistake, Miss Carter!

But the new Sophie wouldn't let something like that phase her. Pulling a face, she mimed at Rupert to keep quiet.

He gave her a grin, and then said as loudly as ever, 'I'll introduce you at coffee-break.'

'What makes you think you're getting a coffee-break?' It was the voice on the microphone again. 'At this rate you'll be lucky to get a cup of tea by nine o'clock tonight. When you're ready...'

Although there was an unexpected hint of humour this time, the final remark clearly meant, I'm waiting for you. The more relaxed atmosphere that Rupert seemed to generate around him tightened again.

However unsure the old Sophie had been about adopting a course of action in the past, she had never been indecisive about people: she knew whom she liked, and whom she didn't like. She didn't, definitely *didn't* like this Alex character, however rich and successful he might be.

She pulled a chair towards the piano as quietly as she could, and sat down to Rupert's left, a little way back from the keyboard. She was coming to a decision about something else: arranging as quick an exit as possible once the recording session had ended. She had no intention whatsoever of meeting Mr Producer Tarrant if she could help it. She was fully prepared to admit that, as far as the job of page turner went, she was not an ideal candidate—he had yet to discover that, of course— but that didn't mean she was to be treated as a brainless minion.

There was a pile of photocopied sheets on top of the piano. Mindful of the microphones, and the awful sarcastic voice, she pointed and raised her eyebrows. Their audience didn't worry Rupert, but he left out the banter this time. 'Yes. This is it. I thought I'd start with something I could play from memory, but since you're here we might as well get some of this over with. Is that all right, Alex?' He was selecting a piece of music as he spoke, and spreading it out on the piano.

'Hello.'

That voice again. Grudgingly she admitted to herself that the deep tone of it really *was* rather attractive when it wasn't being scathing—until it struck her that of course that special quality lent all the more edge to it when it was being nasty, and further confirmed her opinion of the speaker's unpleasantness.

Rupert was talking. 'Is it OK if I switch to one of the other pieces? That was a warm-up.'

'We'll get through that first prelude, if you don't mind, Rupert.' The 'if you don't mind' translated as, I mind even if you don't—you'll do what I say.

Rupert shrugged. 'No problem. I just thought I'd make Sophie work for her money.'

'Right,' said the voice, in a tone that dismissed the pianist's final remark as an irrelevance. This time there was a brief, almost inaudible mutter of conversation between Alex and somebody else—'The recording engineer,' Rupert whispered at her—and then the voice said, 'Ready, Derek? Take three.'

Sophie's nightmare began. First of all, she wasn't sure whether Rupert was playing from memory, or whether he had changed to the piece in front of him, as he had asked. There was no title on the manuscript photocopies. She glanced at him for a clue, but he took no notice of her, sitting in silence, his head bowed, his arms hanging loosely by his sides. Then after a few moments he looked up and began to play. He seemed to be gazing somewhere up into the organ gallery and not at the music at all.

Aware all the time of the invisible Mr Tarrant, she began to feel very nervous. She tried to fit what Rupert was playing to the notes on the pages before him. She half got up when she expected him to have reached somewhere near the end of the second page, and then

sat down again as he ignored her. Then she got up again
as he moved into a more energetic phase; he seemed to
be nodding his head, and she didn't know whether he
meant it for her, or whether it was just part of his
manner. She sat down again.

Finally the piece came to an end. There was a ringing
silence, and then the deep voice on the speaker again.
'We'll do it once more. There were some background
noises in that.'

She looked at her companion guiltily. 'It was my
chair!' she breathed, mindful of the walls and the ears.
'It creaks every time I stand up!'

'What did you want to stand up for?' Rupert demanded, far too loudly. 'I wondered why you were
bobbing around like a cork.'

She felt betrayed once again—the sarcastic Alex could
hear every word.

'I—er—couldn't see the music properly,' she lied, on
sudden inspiration, then tried to sound accusing. 'You
set it up at an impossible angle! I was trying to have a
look at it.' She hoped the voice was listening.

There were several more attempts at the first piece
before the invisible producer was satisfied. His
judgement overrode everyone else's, and when she whispered to Rupert, 'Why do you let him get away with it?'
he merely whispered back,

'Because he's the boss and he knows what he's talking
about—which is more than the rest of us do!'

Reflecting on her newly adopted motto of 'Try
Anything Once', she was forced to the conclusion that
it wasn't such a wise one after all! She'd met Rupert for
a cup of coffee a few days earlier, and they'd exchanged
news, his being chiefly that he was about to make a recording, and hers that she was in the middle of changing
flats, having moved out of one but not yet into the other.

'I'm staying with my father,' she'd explained. 'It's fine
for the moment, but if I get another commission he's

not going to take too kindly to having a huge tapestry frame taking up his sitting-room! I'll be living with a friend from the end of September, but her present lodger can't move out before then.'

At that point they'd discussed her job briefly, and he'd listened to her complaints that large tapestries in need of expert repair paid well when you found them, but were proving very difficult to track down. As a result she was in what could be best described as a cash-flow crisis just at present. It was then he'd suggested she could earn a few extra pounds by turning pages for him at the recording session.

'You'd get paid by the hour. It won't be much, but it'd be fun, and it's better than nothing,' he'd argued. 'There'd be a free meal thrown in too. Don't worry about reading the music—I'm the one who has to do that. Easy as falling off a log.'

Yes. Well. She knew now she'd rather fall off a log any day, given the choice over again. She had learned the piano to a basic level while at school, but he hadn't told her that he'd be playing some very complicated modern stuff where you were lucky if you could recognise anything beyond the first note.

But of course it wasn't really the good-natured Rupert she was worrying about. All the time there was the invisible man behind the microphones, with the cutting edge to his voice. He seemed to be able to convey scathing disapproval in so very few words. But if she could avoid any sort of encounter with him she might become inured to the comments, and the page turning might even improve as it went on.

It didn't. If anything, it got worse. Her next attempt with the photocopied sheets brought them off the stand. Somehow she had become entangled with Rupert' left arm.

Without thinking, she apologised instantly. 'Oh, gosh, sorry—I didn't realise you'd got to the end!' Her words sounded clearly above the piano.

Seconds later the dreaded speaker crackled again, and Alex's voice sliced through the flying notes.

'Hold it, Rupert—what's going on? Somebody——' he made her sound like a moronic alien who had just strayed in '—talked in the middle of that. And what the hell was that crashing noise?'

He sounded so irritated that this time Sophie wished she could sink through the floor. He must know perfectly well it was she who had ruined the 'take'.

Even Rupert sounded conciliatory. 'Just a few technical problems—nothing to worry about. Er—Alex— could I start that again from the beginning? The opening was a bit messy.'

'Didn't seem a lot wrong with it to me.' Curt disapproval. Silence while the speaker was turned off, then, 'No. We've got a lot to get through. Take it from just before the break—and, as your page turner doesn't seem to have grasped the idea yet, perhaps you could make it clear to her that *every sound* is recorded. Ready, Derek? When you're ready, Rupert.'

The engineer's voice said, 'Take thirteen . . .' and Rupert, grimacing at Sophie, launched himself once more into the fiendish jumble of notes.

She nearly gave up in despair many times before the morning was ended. When Rupert had offered her the job, it sounded like easy money. Now she was of the opinion that no sum could compensate for the damage to her nerves.

She was impossibly hungry. She hadn't had time for much breakfast that morning, and her stomach was beginning to complain. She wrapped her arms tightly around her middle, praying that Rupert wouldn't suddenly play a soft passage that would betray every ominous rumble. Luckily Rupert himself asked for a break before the state of her digestion ruined the proceedings yet again.

There was a brief discussion over the microphone, and a general agreement that they should stop for half an hour. Then Alex's voice said, 'Want to come and listen to the recording?'

Her chance to meet a famous record producer—and find out what the sarcastic voice looked like! 'No, thanks,' she said instantly. Her mental image of Alex had supplied him with horns and a tail. To have him treat her face to face with the contempt implied by his comments was an experience she could live without.

'Come on, Sophe,' Rupert encouraged. 'Find out what it's going to sound like on the disc!'

She ignored the 'Sophe', and the face she pulled as she reached under her chair for her shoes had nothing to do with his use of her nickname.

'No, thanks,' she said again. 'I'll die if I don't get some coffee. I'll be back in half an hour—he does mean a whole half-hour, does he? Not ten minutes—or five?' She managed to make that sound pretty sarcastic herself, but she'd forgotten the mikes were still switched on. Before Rupert could reply, the hated voice said, 'Yes— he *does* mean half an hour. Be back here at twelve. Enjoy your coffee!'

He *almost* sounded human that time, but the slight thawing in the tone didn't tempt her to change her mind. She went to the nearest coffee bar, sitting in the window so that she could see Rupert if he passed on a hunt for her. She spent twenty minutes thinking longingly of holidays there was no prospect of having, and, when there was no sign of Rupert, decided she'd better get back. He must have stayed with Derek the engineer, and the unpleasant Alex. She didn't have much interest in Derek, but a perverse curiosity prompted her to speculate about Alex Tarrant, putative owner of the power machine with the embarrassing burglar alarm parked in the square outside. She would have liked to know what he really looked like. Did he suit the car, or, as was all too often the case, was the car merely an attempt to enhance an image none too exciting in itself? He sounded younger than Derek, though not as young as Rupert.

Pity about that corrosive edge to everything he said. He clearly didn't suffer fools gladly, and she was certain he had relegated her to that unflattering category.

Rupert was waiting for her on the steps of the hall when she got back, but to her mingled relief and disappointment—she would have liked a look at the producer from a safe distance—there was no sign of anyone else.

'Where were you?' he demanded. 'I thought you'd be downstairs.'

'Downstairs where?' she asked, puzzled.

'Here—the musicians' coffee bar. There's a sign as big as a billboard on the stairs. When you didn't appear, Alex and I decided you must be titivating in the ladies'—I told him I had a glamorous surprise for him.'

Another nail in the coffin of a fool! she thought grimly. An inept page turner who took a whole half-hour to fiddle with her appearance!

As he spoke, he pushed open the door for her to enter first, and, brushing past him, she caught an unexpected glimpse of a tall, dark-haired man disappearing through the doors to the recording room. She had no more than an impression—slim, broad-shouldered, and casually dressed in a denim shirt and light-coloured trousers. The hand that held the swing-door back as he passed through had been suntanned, and he had worn a gold signet ring on his little finger.

'Who was that?' she asked Rupert quickly.

He hadn't seen him, and shrugged. 'Shortish, fattish and balding?'

She kicked off her shoes, and crossed the floor in her stockinged feet. 'No. Tall, dark and handsome.' The final

adjective was merely part of the cliché; she hadn't seen
the man's features. But she thought it interesting that,
far from quarrelling with the description, Rupert replied
instantly,

'Oh, that was Alex. Want to come and meet him?'

So he *did* suit the car—as far as she could judge from
a passing glimpse, anyway!

She glanced at the microphones doubtfully. 'Hadn't
we better get ready to start? We've had our half an hour.'

He gave her an amused look, but didn't say anything
and sat down again at the piano.

So that was Alex! Not quite what she'd expected...
But now that she'd seen him she could probably fill in
the rest of his character—arrogant, conceited, and patronising towards women, with most of whom, no doubt,
he would have a positively sickening success. Well, here
was one woman at least who could find no charms in
him. In fact the tall, dark arrogant type was so far from
her image of the ideal man that she found the contrast
quite comic. She decided not to redraft her original
picture of him with horns and a tail—after all, in some
stories the devil was supposed to be very good-looking.
She wondered what the record producer would say if he
knew.

After a second session very like the first—the only
plus point being that she developed a better technique
with the pages, so that the rustling was less obvious, and
the photocopies fell off the piano only once—Rupert
declined the invitation to go into the recording room,
and left the hall with her. She was in a hurry to get out
safely.

'There's a good pub along the main road,' he told her.
'But we might have to wait for a table.'

The pub buildings surrounded an old cobbled yard.
There were tables and benches outside, crowded with
dark-suited businessmen.

Inside, it seemed a bit stuffy and dark to Sophie, after
the sunshine. With the hunting prints on the dark, yel-
lowing walls, and the horse brasses hanging by the fire-
place, they could have been miles out in the country, not
thirty yards from a dirty busy London street, the fumes
of the cars forming a kind of tangible haze in the late
summer warmth. She wished again she could have a
holiday a long way away from the city. She seemed to
have been working on and off all year, with no definite
break.

'This place makes me think how much I'd like a few
weeks in the wilds of the country,' she remarked longingly to Rupert as they propped themselves up at the
bar. 'Somewhere I could sit around in *real* country pubs!
But I can't afford to go away anywhere. We used to live
in Sussex when Mum was alive—I was about nine or ten
then, but I still miss it. I'd like a few proper hills and
woods for a change.'

Rupert looked at her thoughtfully. Then he said, 'I
have to go to the Welsh borders in a week—I've got a
recital in someone's house near Leominster, and then I
might stay on for a while. Why not come with me?'

The suggestion surprised her, and she considered it,
sipping her wine. What sort of an invitation was it—did
he see it as an opportunity to further his romantic crush
on her? If so, it wasn't to be encouraged. On the other
hand, there didn't have to be an ulterior motive, and
they'd be sure to have a good time.

'Where would I stay exactly?'

Rupert lit a cigarette. 'At home, with me.'

'But I thought you lived in London!' she exclaimed.

'I only rent a room in the house I'm living in at the
moment. "Home" is the Welsh Marches—scene of innumerable battles between the English and the Welsh in
the bad old days—thick with woods and hills and lit-
tered with castles. If that's wild enough for your country
walks, come with me.'

Sophie's mind was following other tracks just then. 'Do you live on your own?'

He tipped the ash from his cigarette. 'I'd like to impress you with Derrham, and pretend it was all mine, but I suppose I'd better admit that the house and land—all of it—is really my brother's. He has a couple of people living there permanently—Sam Bates and his wife Ellen. Then there are other staff who live on the estate. My mother moved into another house years ago. She's away at the moment, or we could go and see her.'

An estate—and a landowning brother! How many more surprising cards had Rupert got up his sleeve? 'But won't your brother mind? I mean, about a total stranger coming to stay?'

'He won't be there. He's got some business deal cooking that'll keep him away for a few weeks. But even with Vicky around, he'd let me treat the place as my own.'

'Who's Vicky?' she asked curiously.

He pulled a face. 'His ex-wife—she's in the States. You will come, won't you?'

The idea was very tempting, and she could always come back to London again if it didn't seem to be working out. She wouldn't be away long enough to make any difference to her work prospects, she could just about afford the rail fare, and with luck she might even find a client in one of those Welsh border castles if she could persuade Rupert to take her to visit some of them. 'Don't be afraid to have a go!'—*The Successful Businesswoman*, page sixty-three.

'OK...' she agreed slowly. 'Just so long as your brother doesn't object.'

'He won't. I told you,' Rupert assured her, 'I can invite whoever I like. Derrham is my home too. That's settled, then.'

They were both perched on stools at the bar counter, but Rupert seemed reluctant to order any food until they'd got a table.

'Aren't we in a hurry?' she reminded him. 'We don't want to be late back.' The shadow of Alex Tarrant loomed large.

He shrugged. 'It doesn't matter when we'll have the boss with us.'

'The *boss*?' But didn't that mean...?

She had set off the alarm in his car, arrived late for the recording session, interrupted the first 'take' and spoilt innumerable subsequent ones with squeaks, rustles and exclamations, and now she was supposed to be having lunch with him?

She was just about to say she wasn't hungry and had to make an urgent phone call, when a hand gripped her shoulder hard, and she felt herself being swung almost off her bar stool, while, to her astonishment, a voice that sounded all too familiar was addressing her in tones that could have peeled back the wallpaper.

'What the *hell* are you doing here?'

She looked round in blank amazement, as did everyone else within earshot—and found herself staring at Rupert's double.

At least... he was Rupert's double in that he had the same black hair, and he was looking at her with the same blue eyes—almost navy, they were so dark—and he had the same classic perfection of features... But there the resemblance ended. The lines of Rupert's face had a softness about them, almost childish curves in comparison. This man's face seemed to be carved out of granite, and there was a harshness in his expression that was instantly intimidating. And, most disturbing of all, whereas Rupert's good looks left her relatively unmoved, there was something about this stranger that affected her like a sort of magnet that pulled her and repelled her at the same time.

She knew the voice. And if she knew the voice, she knew who the man was—she had discovered enough about him that morning to form an opinion of him, and coming face to face with him did nothing to soften her prejudices; on the contrary, it confirmed them. She told herself she would have been wary of him even if he had greeted her politely. Clearly, Alex Tarrant was every bit as unpleasant as she had suspected—though she couldn't account for the extreme hostility in his manner and expression. And there was no way she could have mistaken the fact that his words were meant for her: he was looking directly at her when he spoke.

But his expression altered subtly even while they stared at each other, and his fingers ceased to dig into her shoulder quite so painfully.

As he took his hand away the angry dark blue gaze transferred itself to Rupert, the open antagonism in his face replaced by something very like accusation.

'Was this by accident or design?' he demanded coldly, but this time he was addressing Rupert.

She glanced at her companion. She couldn't account for his expression either—a look of blank innocence.

'I don't know what you mean, Alex. Let me introduce you to Sophie Carter, who has *very kindly*—' he laid heavy emphasis on the words '—agreed to do the worst job in the world and turn the pages for me.' His manner had altered slightly too, and it was almost as though he was daring the obnoxious Mr Tarrant to be anything but charming to her.

Judging by an instant's expression that flickered across Mr Tarrant's face, there was some mental adjustment going on.

He was standing beside her now. He held out a hand. Normally she would have stood up properly to shake hands with someone she was being introduced to, but, since meeting him in the flesh had confirmed all her earlier judgements of him, she instantly decided that she wouldn't.

'How do you do?' he said, after a moment's hesitation. 'I'm Alex Tarrant. I'm sorry—I mistook you for someone else when I came in just now.'

She withdrew her fingers as soon as he relaxed his grasp; for a few seconds his grip had almost hurt her hand. His apology was no more than a formality, and he made it very obvious—he was already pulling up one of the stools. Not a man to waste his words, but she'd already discovered that this morning.

'Now that you've sworn at her as well, Sophie must think you're some sort of ogre,' Rupert was commenting brightly. 'You've been nasty to her all morning.'

There wasn't even the ghost of a smile on Alex Tarrant's face at that. The blue eyes narrowed, and he gave her a keen look. She had a feeling he was taking her in now as the person she really was—Sophie Carter, warts and all. It didn't make her feel any better.

'So you're the one who can't read music, are you?' It was the sort of opening insult she might have expected.

Rupert cut in before she could open her mouth to reply. 'Come on, Alex, be fair—even you couldn't have managed some of those double pages stuck together with Sellotape!'

Alex Tarrant was still looking at her very attentively. Too attentively, she thought. It amounted to a rude stare. It made her feel very uncomfortable, as though something were crawling about under her skin. She attempted to return the stare, her brown eyes full of hostility.

He was too young for the few threads of silver in his dark hair to pass unremarked, though the lines etched lightly on his face—the furrows between his strongly marked brows and the lines either side of his mouth—suggested a man of some experience. He was the kind who turned heads wherever he went, but not just on account of his undeniable good looks, enhanced by a

perfect tan—nor his contemptuous manner, for that
matter! There was something powerful, almost
dangerous about him—again the devil image came to
mind.

'How long have you known Rupert?' he asked, ignoring her companion's remark.

She shrugged. 'A few months—since the beginning of
this summer.' She sounded almost sullen. She hadn't
meant to, exactly, but he hadn't bothered to be particularly polite to her. Perhaps her manner might force him
to soften his.

'I'm surprised we haven't met before. Have you been
keeping her hidden deliberately, Rupert?'

There was a kind of undercurrent to his words which
carried them far from the obvious gallant remark a man
might make who took her for Rupert's new girlfriend.
What *was* this about? There was no reason they should
have met before. She didn't move in the same circles as
Alex Tarrant, and until she had turned up at the studio
that morning she had had no idea Rupert was even acquainted with a record producer. In fact there was a
curious undercurrent to the whole conversation. She felt
as though she was being carried along by it against her
will, and she didn't like where it was taking her.

Rupert's eyes were assessing her when he said abruptly, 'I've invited Sophie to stay at Derrham...'

She sensed, rather than saw, a reaction in Alex beside
her.

But Rupert's next announcement was an anticlimax.
She supposed she had guessed it the moment she had
seen Alex Tarrant face to face, and ever since she had
been trying hard not to put a very unpleasant two and
two together to make an even nastier four.

Rupert turned to her, his eyes this time on the man
sitting beside him.

'Alex is my brother,' he said sweetly.

CHAPTER TWO

BROTHERS...

'You look very alike,' she offered lamely, after the pause had lengthened to a point where it was becoming embarrassing.

If she hadn't already changed her mind about going to Derrham, the glance with which Alex Tarrant greeted that remark would have caused her to alter her decision on the spot. Never mind about 'Try anything once'— there was no question of staying at Derrham now, whatever the prospect of tapestries in need of repair. She'd make some excuse and get out of it; she would no longer be accepting her friend's hospitality, but, indirectly, his obnoxious brother's.

She had guessed the relationship the moment she'd seen Alex, of course, and watching the brothers sitting side by side emphasised the similarities rather than diminished them. Superficially, Alex was an older, harder version of Rupert. She glanced at him out of the corner of her eye, when she thought he wasn't looking. 'Collect your facts', *The Successful Businesswoman* had instructed. Right... Alex Tarrant: divorced, though wife possibly still around—Rupert's words earlier seemed to imply she might put in the occasional appearance; in sole possession of a house and land on the Welsh borders; surprisingly young, despite the hint of silver in his hair— only thirty-one if the newspapers were to be believed. He was apparently rich and successful, and most certainly arrogant—he gave the impression of being the sort of person who had never taken orders from anybody.

25

Why on earth hadn't Rupert told her at the very beginning who he was? She couldn't possibly have guessed, just from their names on a list, that they were so closely related—Rupert might have changed his name for professional reasons, or they could have different fathers.

But what was really puzzling was the way in which Alex had mistaken her for someone else. His first words had been spoken before he reached the bar, and she had had her back to him. Her long blonde hair and high heels were as unremarkable as those of any similar young woman in London, but a partial glimpse of her face reflected in the mirror behind the bar counter could have convinced him for a few seconds that she was—well, who exactly?

She was sure Rupert knew. And Alex was well aware that his brother had seen the resemblance, hence his accusing look. He thought that in some way Rupert had set this up—why else ask a page turner along who 'couldn't read music'? The pianist could be very charming and good-natured, but there was sometimes a malicious streak to his humour. She didn't fancy being caught in the middle of some devious game he was playing with his brother.

'Sophie?'

Rupert broke in on her speculations, and she became abruptly aware that she had been staring at Alex and that there had been another awkward silence.

'You *are* coming to stay, aren't you?' Rupert demanded.

She glanced at him and then looked back very directly, and very consciously, at Alex. 'Your brother kindly invited me,' she said, 'but I'm afraid I'll have work to do then.'

The pianist protested at once, 'But I thought you said you didn't have any work just now!'

Dear Rupert! She might be indecisive, but she wasn't uninventive.

'I—er—forgot about something my father said he'd fix up for me. It'll have to be that week if it happens at all... After that the client will be going away.' Alex had pulled up a bar stool next to hers, so that she was sandwiched between the two men. They were both looking at her, but she felt overwhelmingly aware of Alex. Despite her instinctive dislike of him, she had to admit to herself that he was a stunningly attractive man. His knee was only inches from hers, and she couldn't help wondering how much of his body was covered by that wonderful golden tan. His blue denim shirt was open at the throat, and she could see the dark chest hair that began below the bones of his neck.

'Do you work for your father?' he asked, and she shifted uncomfortably under that hard gaze. She changed her position on the stool, so that there was a greater distance between them, and explained briefly about the flat situation, and her father.

'Are your parents divorced?'

'No. Mum died when I was ten.'

'Brothers or sisters?'

What was this—an inquisition? The peculiar quality of his attention was unnerving.

'No.'

For the first time, she thought she detected a flicker of interest in those cold blue eyes. 'Would you say that you suffered in any way by being an only daughter brought up by her father?'

She looked at him in surprise. What an extraordinary question from a virtual stranger! And an implication that she was spoilt?

'Certainly not!' she replied firmly. 'And Dad and I are still very good friends, if that proves anything.'

'So what do you do for a living, Sophie, apart from turning pages?'

She wished she could believe his interest was in Sophie Carter, and not in some purely personal line he was pursuing. This time she was sure she could detect a patronising sneer in his tone. *The Successful Businesswoman*, page forty-three: 'Don't let him get away with it!' Though that wasn't something she would have done anyway.

She looked at him levelly. 'I mend things... Who do you work for?'

He assessed her in a manner she described to herself as extremely insolent. His eyes took in her long, palely tanned legs, high heels and her carefully manicured bright red fingernails.

'Myself.'

'But don't you work for the record company?'

'I own it.'

Oh. She couldn't claim to have scored in that little round!

He was still assessing her. 'What sort of things do you mend—back axles? Combine harvesters? People's hot-water tanks?'

From someone else that might have been amusing, but from him she was certain it was meant as an insult; he thought her vain and silly, his opinion no doubt reinforced by the belief that she had spent the entire coffee-break earlier that day improving her appearance in the ladies' at the recording studios. The temptation to mislead him, for Rupert's entertainment and her own private satisfaction, was too strong to resist.

'Victorian lace handkerchiefs for antique shops.' There was a grain of truth in it—she had once repaired some antique lace for a client—but the answer sounded every bit as lightweight as she had hoped.

'A valuable contribution to society.' The sarcasm, despite the quiet tone in which he uttered it, made even Rupert blink.

Alex's antagonism towards her was blatant, and with every new exchange her conviction deepened that the mysterious undercurrents were still tugging away beneath the surface conversation, and that there was something going on between the two brothers concerning her. She was just wondering if she should jump into the uneasy silence which followed with a defence of her supposed vocation in life, when a new expression, which could only be described as a smirk, crossed Rupert's face.

She guessed he had thought of some way to score against Alex—but if she had had any idea of the complications that were to follow she would have left the pub there and then.

'I'm glad you approve, Alex,' said his brother smoothly. 'Sophie and I are getting married.'

'Rupert!' Her choking protest was intended to prompt an instant retraction from him, but in the act of sipping her wine she was forced to put her glass down again very quickly. Her subsequent fit of coughing interrupted further remarks from any of them.

At his brother's announcement, Alex's eyebrows had drawn together instantly in a frown of disapproval. His glance flicked from Sophie to her companion and back again. There was no way of telling whether he believed in the engagement or not, but one thing was obvious— if the expression 'looking daggers' could have any literal truth, both she and Rupert would have been bloodied corpses right there in front of the bar. Rupert, however, was unperturbed and instantly turned her protest to his advantage. 'Don't take any notice of Sophie,' he advised his brother in calm tones. 'She wanted to keep it a secret a bit longer, but I thought you ought to be the first to know.'

'Thank you.' Alex's tone was disappointingly neutral.

About to open her mouth once more in instant denial, Sophie suddenly thought better of it. What private amusement Rupert got out of all this was known only to himself, but, still smarting from his brother's dismissive attitude towards her, she was very tempted now to give in to impulse and play along with him. It would serve Alex right if he did have a sleepless night over the prospect of his brother's forthcoming marriage! She would never have to encounter him again after today, and it was her one small opportunity of revenge for his unpleasantness to her.

Alex was watching her again, although his next words were for his brother. 'You're a dark horse, Rupert. When did all this romance start to bloom?'

'Oh, Sophe and I have been seeing each other for some time.'

'And how long have you been engaged?'

Sophie felt her hackles rise. He had no right to cross-question them!

Rupert's reply was offhand. 'Not long. I asked her the other night, didn't I, Sophes?'

'Yes, *Roops*.'

Rupert gave an amused snort at that, but an almost imperceptible tightening of the lips was Alex's only re-action, and his unspoken disapproval fuelled her desire to make the most of her chance to get her own back. On impulse, she turned fully towards Alex, her brown eyes bright with inspiration. Try anything once.

'Roops is *such* a wonderful pianist! I'm amazed he isn't world-famous. It must be *marvellous* to have such a talented brother!' she gushed. And then more confidingly, 'I do hope this recording is a good one. Do you know his last record really wasn't very well edited at all? There were actually *dozens* of notes missing from it!' She had no idea which company had been concerned with the production of Rupert's first and only recording to date, or who had been the producer involved, but she couldn't help hoping it was the man sitting only inches from her.

One dark eyebrow rose in scepticism. 'Surely not "dozens"!' he mimicked her.

'Oh, yes,' she assured him gaily. 'Roops said it was really awful, and it would be dreadful for him if it happened again!'

'Indeed it would,' Alex agreed so blandly that she had no way of knowing whether the remark had hit home or not. She didn't quite dare turn round to look at Rupert yet. Alex glanced at his watch. 'If we're going to have lunch, I suggest we get on with it. There's a table free in the corner.'

There was something very final about the way he said that, and she found herself going along with the suggestion even before she was aware of it—Rupert, too, obediently transferred himself to the table in question. Then she resented the way Alex had taken charge; it was as though they were still in the recording studio.

Her small attempt at asserting her independence was to complain that she didn't like sitting with her back to the room.

'Fuss-pot,' Rupert commented as he made way for her, and she could see from the look on Alex's face that he shared that sentiment. But whereas Rupert's remark had been in jest, his brother's opinion was seriously held. There had been something very like a contemptuous gleam in his eye just then. It was only too obvious he liked his women meek and docile, the sort who did what they were told!

A free meal had been one of the inducements offered by Rupert, and the menu was varied and appetising, but, mindful of a particularly glamorous black dress she intended to wear to a friend's party at the end of the week, she decided she'd better stick to salad. She couldn't afford to put on even an ounce.

As she picked at her lettuce, she was aware of Alex's disapproving eye on her again. 'You don't look as though you need to diet, Sophie.'

A finicky eater—another black mark! There was no end to her shortcomings in his eyes!

She smiled winsomely at him, as though she took it as a compliment. Her determination to give him a very uneasy run for his money didn't falter. 'I've got this *fabulous* dress!' she enthused. 'I'm wearing it to a party, and it's so tight I just might pop out of it if I'm not careful!' She was pleased to find she could manage the sort of giggle which made even Rupert wince. But, before he could say anything, she rushed on, 'I'm so looking forward to seeing Derrham, Alex—it's such a pity it can't be this time. Roops and I plan to go down there whenever we can after we're married. I've got lots of ideas for decorating and things like that, and we could have house parties and entertain lots of friends. You must know *thousands* of interesting people! I don't mind cooking for them or anything, if your wife's not around—Roops says I'm a wonderful cook, don't you, darling?' She gave him one of her sideways glances, and Rupert's nose was buried suddenly in his handkerchief. She'd been a good actress at school, and she'd forgotten what fun it was.

'Thank you, that won't be necessary.' Not a flicker of an expression had crossed Alex's face, but his reply had all the warmth of a bucket of ice. 'I have a housekeeper who does the cooking. We don't entertain much these days.'

The quality of his reply daunted even Sophie, and Rupert, recovering from his sneezing choke or whatever it was, quickly cut in, changing the subject abruptly.

The talk was of recording and the business of the day after that, and she got the distinct impression she wasn't being allowed to say anything by either man.

She didn't have a chance to talk to Rupert privately until they left the pub. Alex, with a glance at his watch, announced that he was going on ahead. 'I've got an important phone call to Germany before we start up again.' He gave a disapproving glance at Sophie's high heels. 'You two follow on as fast as you can. See you back at the studio!'

He strode away from them, conspicuous for his height, a strikingly handsome man. She saw two girls turn round after him in the street. They nudged each other and giggled, then turned to look again.

If you knew what he's really like, she thought acidly, you wouldn't be half so impressed! But she had a sneaking feeling of disappointment that he had left them so abruptly. That spark of danger had gone out of the air.

Once he was safely out of earshot, she attacked Rupert on the subject of their engagement.

'Whatever possessed you to tell him that?' she began. 'For some reason he's taken an instant dislike to me—it really sticks in his guts that I'm a prospective sister-in-law, and he doesn't miss an opportunity to make that obvious. I suppose he thinks I'm cradle snatching!'

Rupert gave a contemptuous snort. 'Rubbish—you're still an absolute baby and you don't look a day over seventeen! Anyway, there's not that much difference between us——'

She didn't want to pursue that in case he took it as encouragement, and cut in with, 'I know what it is—I wouldn't be good enough for the likes of the Tarrants and the Strettons! Well, all I can say is, thank goodness there's only this afternoon to get through—I'm not used to being insulted with quite such dedication to the cause! What on earth are you up to?'

'Oh, come on, Sophe——'

'Don't call me that!'

'All right. What's all this about not coming to Derrham? I thought we'd agreed.'

'I'm not going anywhere I might meet that man again!'

'You won't. I promise you. Alex is a mega business tycoon—he doesn't have time to loaf around at Derrham. He'll be in Munich fixing up a take-over bid for a recording company.'

It took almost the whole way back to the square for him to persuade her, but she gave in in the end.

'Just so long as your brother Mr Tarrant isn't within a hundred miles of the place,' she warned him.

Rupert grinned. 'Do I deduce from all this that you're not instantly enamoured of the handsome Alex?'

She didn't need to search for words. 'I think he's the rudest, most unpleasant man I've *ever* met. I'm surprised he has any friends at all if that's his usual behaviour—that is, if he *has* any friends! And if I didn't need the money so badly, you'd be dropping your own photocopies off the piano this afternoon!'

She took the precaution of loitering outside the studio until she was quite sure Alex was out of the way before she went back to her chair at the piano. This time she checked the page turns in advance. Rupert had warned her that the first piece was very fast, and that there was a story to it.

'It's called the "Mephisto Waltz",' he had told her. 'The devil tunes up his violin one night at an inn. He starts to play for some lovers, and catches everyone up in the magic of his music.'

'So the devil calls the tune, as you might say?'

'You might. The devil plays, and you dance.'

That fitted her image of Alex to perfection! With those dark, magnetic good looks he would be the ideal candidate for the part of the devil in a story—and while he was around he unquestionably called the tune.

She managed to avoid the producer completely during the afternoon session, and left the hall at the end with scarcely a glimpse of him; it was a relief to think that that was positively the last she would ever see of him.

Derek, the engineer, appeared very briefly just as she was leaving. He was the short, fat, and balding character Rupert had referred to earlier, and she thought he made a very telling remark.

'Good work, Sophie,' he said as they shook hands. It was nice to be appreciated! 'You had one of the most thankless jobs of the lot, and the most nerve-racking. Glad it wasn't me—I only had the second nastiest job, trying to keep the maestro happy!'

'Oh, come on,' said Rupert modestly. 'I'm not that hard to please!'

Derek laughed. '*You're* not,' he agreed with emphasis, 'but Alex is the devil. Still, that's what makes him the best in the business, so we mustn't complain!'

Why mustn't we, Sophie thought, when he makes everyone's life a misery in the process? But she didn't say it. At that moment she caught sight of the producer emerging from the recording room, and was halfway to the exit in seconds, speeded on her way by the knowledge that Alex had seen her—for an instant their eyes had met. The sparks had been travelling in both directions.

Although her hasty escape ensured that she wouldn't have to meet Alex Tarrant again, it didn't stop her thinking about him, and for several days afterwards she found herself resentfully banishing his image from her thoughts. It seemed to appear in her mind unbidden: there he would be, without any warning, dark, handsome and dangerous, looking at her with those contemptuous blue eyes, and she'd find herself hating him all over again.

If there had been the slightest chance of his turning up at Derrham during her projected stay there she would never have taken up the invitation. She rang Rupert a couple of days after the recording just to make sure, and succeeded in getting him to agree to meet her at the station. She also got the Derrham phone number for emergencies.

'By the way, does Alex still think we're engaged?' she asked while she wrote it down.

'Presumably. He hasn't said anything about it, but I haven't seen him since the recording. He's been very busy. Oh, by the way, if you're going to be my fiancée I want to show you off, so bring something smart to wear—I've got a recital you can come to, and there's a party afterwards!'

'But we can't play tricks on the whole county!' she protested. 'There wouldn't be any point in it!'

'Oh, I'm not going to tell anybody about it or anything,' he said airily. 'But you never know, the rumour might get about.'

She thought of something. 'Rupert—this phone number. Supposing I lose it? Where is it I'm trying to get to exactly?'

'Derrham Castle.'

For the whole of three seconds her mouth was open. 'Derrham *Castle*?'

His reply was offhand. 'Don't sound too impressed. It's a very second-class one—no moat or drawbridge or anything like that. OK, Sophes, I have to go. See you soon.'

And typically, before she could open her mouth to voice her usual protest, he'd rung off. Perhaps he would get bored with the nicknames in the end if they failed to produce the desired effect. Really, sometimes he could be very childish.

The idea of the Welsh Marches with its line of guardian castles appealed to her. Lucky Rupert—and lucky Alex Tarrant—to have a lifestyle that could make the most of the two worlds; all that London could have to offer, as well as a splendid home in such idyllic country. Obviously, neither of them had to worry about where the next penny was coming from.

There was a wildly romantic streak in Sophie which had led her into taking up her unusual occupation, no matter how precarious the living she made from it. She took infinite pains with her work and for her every old tapestry was a vital link with the past; while she stitched, she liked to imagine the people who had made it. Perhaps there would be a tapestry or two at Derrham for her to look at, but it was a pity she was on such bad terms with their owner.

When she arrived at Leominster station there was no sign of Rupert. To her dismay, the station seemed to have closed down, although the trains still stopped there.

In the absence of any better plan, she decided to wait for a while to see if Rupert would turn up. She'd told him the train she was catching, but he wasn't renowned for his punctuality. She was relieved when a battered old station wagon drew up, but, instead of Rupert, a tall, well-dressed woman got out and disappeared round the back of the furniture dealer's that now occupied one of the old station outbuildings. There were three noisy dogs in her car that barked hysterically until she returned carrying a small stool, its carved legs sticking out of an inadequate wrapping of brown paper. She glanced across at Sophie, and then looked at her again rather keenly, as though she thought she knew her and then decided she didn't.

'No taxis here, y'know,' she informed her briskly. 'I'll give you a lift if you're going in my direction.'

Sophie smiled at her. 'Thanks. But someone's coming for me.'

The woman made a sound like 'Hmph!', lifted a hand in Sophie's direction in the manner of a royal wave, and got into the car, pushing the stool across into the front seat. The station wagon disappeared in a cloud of exhaust fumes, the noise of the engine drowning the barking of the dogs.

Sophie spent the rest of the time sitting on a station bench, idly speculating on the chances of coming across an old tapestry in need of repair while she was at Derrham. *The Successful Businesswoman* had stressed the importance of snatching at every opportunity, and following up every likely lead. Perhaps she had been too casual about that in the past, though she'd always known that in her profession work came from recommendation. If she was going to make any sort of name for herself at restoration, she couldn't afford to lose any more chances. Her experience was too limited as yet, although she had worked on several notable pieces.

Rupert arrived after a further ten minutes in a smart new Range Rover.

'Sorry I'm late,' he announced, with no hint of repentance. 'My car wouldn't start and I had to borrow this from one of the estate workers. Hop in.'

He drove at what she considered reckless speed through the narrow country lanes, taking a tortuous route, and it struck her that Derrham might be very hard to find if you were a stranger to the area.

'Just one thing before we get there,' she began, a little nervously. 'Your brother—he hasn't changed his plans or anything since we talked on the phone? The last thing I'd want is for him to turn up and find me here! He doesn't approve of me.'

'Nonsense,' said Rupert firmly. 'He's just stunned by your beauty. Someone as gauche and unsophisticated as Alex doesn't know how to react. Now in my case...' The idea was so incongruous that she laughed. 'Alex— gauche? If you'd told me he was the last womaniser in London I'd be prepared to believe you, even though I haven't had personal experience of it! He's every inch sophisticated.' She threw away the next line. 'Quite intimidating, I imagine, if you happen to be impressed by that type.' That managed to sound very successfully offhand, from someone who had been only too aware of the intimidation aspects. What she wasn't going to admit, even to herself, was that a man like Alex Tarrant was way out of her experience. One glance from those scornful blue eyes, and he could have reduced her to a blushing schoolgirl—if she'd let him.

'If he's so dishy, why aren't *you* at his feet?'

Her smile faded with her amusement. 'I told you before; he's arrogant and rude—very far from being my ideal man!'

'So who is?' He glanced across at her.

'I like men who wear comfortable old jerseys and reading glasses. The sort of men you can trust!'

'That rules out Alex, eh?'

'And you, Rupert Stretton!' she retorted. 'As far as your brother is concerned, I may not be the world's greatest intellectual, but I do object to being treated as though I'd got a head full of feathers.'

'Don't worry about it,' Rupert soothed. 'His mental computer has you keyed in as somebody else, and is programmed to act accordingly.'

She thought instantly of her meeting with him. 'Who do you mean exactly by "somebody else"?' she demanded.

'Oh, nothing,' he replied dismissively. 'Look, there's Derrham now.'

Derrham Castle, when they arrived at it, was even better than she'd expected. As the Range Rover took them through the tall iron gates, she caught a glimpse of towers rising from the billows of green oaks that overflowed the little valley. A short drive wound down the valley floor and then up the gentle rise on which the castle stood—and it *was* a castle, despite Rupert's 'second-class' label.

It had four solid round bastions—great fortified towers set at each corner—and castellations along the battlements of the roof. The main house section in the centre, however, had a fine old porch and leaded Jacobean windows.

All Sophie said was, 'Gosh!'

'Not the sort of thing you'd want to defend against a serious army, is it?' Rupert commented. 'Not much scope for boiling oil to fry your enemies or anything.'

'I think it's wonderful!' she exclaimed. '*Did* anyone have to defend it?'

He was getting out of the Range Rover. 'Don't ask me—I'm only a musician. You'd have to ask Alex about that some time—if you could bring yourself to speak to him. The Tarrants have owned it since the seventeenth century.'

She was delighted by Derrham and everything in it. Despite its grand exterior, inside it struck her as a real home. The polished wood floors were covered by old oriental rugs, and there were cabinets full of beautiful china, and portraits on the walls. A glimpse of the library revealed a room lined from floor to ceiling with leather-bound books, and set with comfortable armchairs round an old hearth with iron firedogs for the logs. A grand piano stood in front of the window, piled with books of music, and everywhere were flowers.

Later, in the enormous kitchen with its copper pans and stone-flagged floor, she met Mrs Bates, who had been cooking a supper for them, and was about to put on her coat and go home to the Lodge for the night.

Sophie entered the kitchen with Rupert just behind her, and, although she was prepared to meet the housekeeper, it was quite clear that Ellen Bates hadn't been prepared to meet her. The look of absolute astonishment—almost shock—on her face at the sight of her was followed by a quick puzzled frown. Sophie turned back to Rupert in surprise.

'This is Sophie Carter, Ellen,' he said quickly. 'She's staying here with me for a couple of weeks, as I told you.' Ellen gave a half-smile and rubbed her hands on her apron. 'I'm sorry, miss,' she apologised. 'You surprised me for a second there when you came in so sudden.' All the while the older woman's eyes were thoughtful, studying her. Then she turned to Rupert. 'Would it be all right if I got off home now? Only I haven't made a start on Sam's meal yet, and time's getting on.'

After Ellen Bates had gone, Rupert offered to show Sophie her room.

'You haven't told Mrs Bates we're engaged, or anything silly like that, have you?' she asked suspiciously, on their way upstairs. The housekeeper's reaction had been very odd. Another one, perhaps, who took her for somebody else?

'Of course not. But she's got a good sense of humour. She'd see the joke.'

'What joke?' she demanded. It had to have something to do with Alex.

But he declined to enlighten her.

She examined her bedroom with interest once he had left her to unpack. Somebody had spent quite a lot of money on redecorating Derrham, judging from the rooms she had seen so far. The furnishings were in excellent taste, and she remembered the act she had put on in the pub; her brash offer to redecorate the castle seemed doubly insulting now, faced with the beauty of the reality. Who had been the designer—Alex's wife?

She went to bed that night thinking about the unamiable Alex. He had been given everything a man could wish for in life—a beautiful home, land, money, and, as if that weren't enough, exceptional good looks and talent. It was a pity he was such an unpleasant character. In fact, if there was one thing that diminished her pleasure in her unexpected holiday, it was the nagging thought that he would suddenly turn up to spoil it all. Like the devil in paradise...

She and Rupert spent the weekend exploring some of the surrounding countryside. She enjoyed the sightseeing, but secretly she would have preferred to stay at Derrham. In her eyes, the old castle had far more

treasures to show than the neighbouring towns. She had
found two superb Flemish tapestries—one in the dining-
room, in good condition, and the second on the wall of
the ancient stairwell, with one section in a very poor
state of repair. Her professional eye at once noted the
flaws. If something wasn't done to it soon, the repair
would become very difficult—and very expensive indeed.
She mentioned it to Rupert, but he showed little interest.

'It's up to Alex,' he said. 'I suppose he knows it's
falling to pieces. He'll get round to it eventually. Why
don't you offer to mend it for him? Write to him, and
send him an estimate. He might take you up on it.' In
her present impecunious state, it was a pity she couldn't
do just that. But after the way she and Alex had struck
sparks off each other, there could be no question of it.

Everything contributed to the idyllic existence in which
she found herself until Sunday evening.

Rupert was giving her an impromptu concert all to
herself in the library, and at her request was playing again
the Liszt piece she thought of as 'the devil's tune'. It
was inextricably associated in her mind with Alex now.

Rupert hadn't finished playing when, as though con-
jured by the music, there was the sound of tyres on the
gravel of the drive, and the low purr of a powerful car
engine. He broke off abruptly, getting up to look out of
the window, and then turned to meet the question in her
eyes—he didn't need to say anything for her heart to
give an uncomfortable thud. He looked both surprised
and strangely expectant. She knew it—she just knew it!
'It's your brother, isn't it?'

He nodded.

All her disappointment fuelled her vehemence. 'But
you said he wouldn't be here!' She couldn't help an instant suspicion that Rupert had set this up in some way
for his own amusement. 'Alex doesn't want me staying

in his house—he could scarcely bring himself to be polite to me in London!'

'Nonsense,' said Rupert shortly. 'You're my fiancée, remember? Anyway, Alex doesn't mind me having friends to stay. Why should he mind about you particularly?'

'You tell me!' she said crossly. She resented the way her heart seemed to be beating faster—it was almost as though she was preparing to face a real ordeal. 'Fight or flight'—that was what adrenalin was for, wasn't it? Again, she was indecisive. It wasn't her nature to give in easily, but running away definitely had the stronger appeal just at the moment. Alex Tarrant was a loathsome character.

She got up abruptly. 'You're up to something, Rupert—trying to score off Alex in some private game! If that's the case, you can count me out!'

'Nonsense,' he said again, and started to play the piano. 'Sit down. You're making me nervous, hovering about like that.'

Still unsure, she perched on the very edge of her chair, but it would look foolish if she bolted now and Alex intercepted her in the hall.

It was only a matter of seconds before he came into the room, but it seemed to her as though she were awaiting a sentence of execution. She just knew in her bones that the amusing, easy time she was having with Rupert would all be spoilt now Alex had arrived.

Alex Tarrant only had to appear in a room for the air around him to pulse with vital energy—she imagined that she could feel the shock-waves as he came through the door. She was struck again by his dark good looks, set off by the flattering tan. She knew he was a handsome man, but she hadn't dwelt on the idea of him so much in terms of his appearance as of his character; it was relatively easy to write him off when he was no more than an abstract bundle of unpleasant reactions and at-

titudes. But the living, breathing reality was much harder
to cope with. His eyes took her in immediately, a flash
of surprise lighting them an intense blue, as though he
hadn't expected to see her there. But his first words were
for Rupert.

'What's this—an exclusive concert?'

'What happened to your take-over bid for that record
company in Munich?' Rupert asked, ignoring the remark
and still playing. 'If you're not careful, they'll be re-
ferring you to the Monopolies Commission!'

'I've postponed the final meeting while they get their
act together...' Alex sounded irritated and dismissive of
it at once. Clearly the company wasn't meeting his stan-
dards. Then he turned to her, and took a stride in her
direction.

She got up quickly before he could reach her. She had
hated the way his height had dominated her before, and
she wasn't going to give him the advantage this time.
What would he say? She held out her hand, and again
felt that powerful grip close round her fingers, though
not quite so crushingly as before. Such a firm handshake from anyone else might have been reassuring—
from him she was sure it was calculated to intimidate.

'The page turner,' he said. 'Hello again.' Repressing
an unaccountable little shiver—resentment that he hadn't
registered her as Rupert's 'fiancée'?—she noted once
more the deep, attractive tones of his voice. 'Welcome
to Derrham. I hope Rupert's been looking after you.'

She couldn't fault that as a hospitable greeting, though
he sounded rather cool, but she suspected the look on
his face, which was enigmatic, masked a dislike that
equalled her own.

'Hello,' she said stiffly. 'Thank you—I've been having
a wonderful time.'

Given their mutual antagonism, combined with the
embarrassing fiction that she was Rupert's future wife,

and her consciousness of the act she had put on when he had last met her, her reply inevitably sounded stilted.

His expression made her think of a handsome Roman statue she'd seen somewhere—sculpted with all the lines of character except humour—and now, although one side of his mouth curved in something resembling a smile, his eyes didn't change. 'Tell Mrs Bates if there's anything you want. Rupert suffers from the delusion that the house runs itself. It never occurs to him to ask if the guests are comfortable. And on that subject, would either of you like a drink?'

She hadn't exactly expected to be ordered from the house, never to darken the doors again, but she hadn't imagined Alex assuming the role of perfect host for her benefit either. Had he decided he'd better make the best of a bad job for his brother's sake? She was surprised and suspicious. It was unlikely that he had revised his first impressions of her.

She wished heartily Rupert hadn't thought up that stupid engagement just to score an obscure point. Alex would have to find out the truth eventually, and the longer the charade went on, the more difficult it would become. She hoped she would be well out of his way when he did discover it.

But there was no need to make an issue of the engagement yet. Who knows? she asked herself. By tomorrow morning Rupert and I could have had a mythical row, and I could have thrown my mythical ring right back in his face—I could even be catching the first train back to London!

CHAPTER THREE

SOPHIE would have turned up to supper in her jeans, if she hadn't met Ellen Bates in the corridor outside the dining-room, carrying a tray laden with silver cutlery. Sophie stopped to open the dining-room door for her, and then gasped in amazement.

'Who's coming to dinner?'

'It's in your honour, I expect,' the housekeeper told her with a smile. 'Mr Alex told me to set it properly. When he's here with Rupert, they both eat in the kitchen. They only use this room when there are guests.'

She too had eaten with Rupert in the kitchen, and she was instantly sceptical about Alex's motives: all this was hardly in her *honour*! The long oak table was set with silver, crystal, and snowy-white damask napkins, and there were branched candlesticks and flowers—but only three places were laid. After her performance in the pub, he was testing her. Perhaps he hoped she would get muddled with her forks, or lick her knife, or blow her nose in her table napkin, thus putting herself indisputably beyond the Tarrant-Stretton pale.

In some moods, she might have been tempted to give him a good run for his money, and behaved outrageously. Alex Tarrant seemed to have the most extraordinary effect on her, and she didn't need much prompting to try to get the better of him. To a certain extent, it was a defence mechanism, but in his company she always had the feeling she was skating on very thin ice; it was challenging and exciting, and she couldn't resist it, even though she suspected that the consequences—if the ice broke and she fell through—would be awful.

She was almost disappointed that so far he had been faultlessly polite. Although he hadn't spent long with her, he could hardly be charged with wilfully neglecting her—the telephone had rung almost continually since his arrival.

'You wouldn't think I paid some of these people to make the decisions for me, would you?' he remarked with an edge of exasperation after the fifth interruption. 'And I want no well-worn witticisms from you, Rupert Stretton, about the price of being a dictator!'

Rupert had opened his mouth. He shut it again.

After a brief consultation of *The Successful Businesswoman*, she reviewed her own strategy with regard to Mr Mega-success Tarrant, and the awkward position she had got herself into as his brother's future wife. It would make things more difficult for him if she gave him no ammunition, and he'd have a much harder time getting rid of a prospective sister-in-law in whom he could find no obvious flaws. It was up to him to account for any inconsistencies with her earlier brash manner; she was under no obligation to explain her behaviour.

She changed for dinner, but her matching scarlet top and skirt, though eye-catching, and showing her figure to advantage, were anything but tasteless. Had she been genuinely anxious for the approval of Rupert's critical brother, she couldn't have done better and, examining her appearance in the mirror, she was pleased with the result. There was no false modesty about Sophie—there were times when she passed as merely another pretty girl, and times when she was more than that. This was definitely one of the latter.

'You look rather stunning, Sophe,' was Rupert's comment when she came downstairs. Significantly, Alex said nothing, but his eyes took her in immediately, and she was aware of his gaze—thoughtful rather than critical—more than once before they went in to the dining-room. Both men had changed out of the clothes they had been wearing earlier, but there was nothing formal in the appearance of either, and she felt relieved that she had guessed the mood of the evening correctly.

Judging from the way Alex watched her at dinner, her suspicions of his underlying motives were well founded. She was sure now that the formality of the surroundings, not guaranteed to put anyone at their ease, was calculated to intimidate the prospective addition to the Tarrant-Stretton clan.

When a phone call took Rupert from the room, her heart sank. That aura of power that surrounded his brother seemed more than ever a direct threat to her. It was the first time she had ever been alone with him, and she had suspected from the moment they entered the dining-room that, given an opportunity, that unaccountable hostility he felt towards her was going to get an airing, if she didn't seize the advantage first.

But even as the thought occurred to her, and she opened her mouth to ask him how soon he would be leaving Derrham, it was too late!

'Tell me, Sophie,' he was saying, before she could get out so much as her first syllable, 'is it stereos you're after, or just a joy-ride in a powerful car?' There was accusation in his tone as he sat back in his chair, wine glass in hand, and there was a hard challenge in his eyes. He hadn't wasted a second—Rupert was scarcely out of the room!

His attitude was clear, but his words had made no sense to her. '*What*?' She stared at him blankly.

'My car alarm,' he prompted smoothly. 'You might remember it went off outside the studios the other day?'

'Oh, yes?' *Oh, no*!

'Someone in a nearby house gave me a very interesting description of a young woman behaving suspiciously... Long blonde hair and red high heels, I think she said.'

There was no point in denying it—she hadn't done any damage. She resisted the impulse to evade his gaze, meeting it with an answering challenge. 'I'd have the alarm mended if I were you,' she advised briskly. 'You could spend your whole life rushing outside to turn it off! I just happened to be walking past.'

The expression in his eyes didn't change. 'That's not what my informant said. She seemed to think you were examining the contents through the driver's window. What exactly *were* you doing? The alarm is faulty, but it doesn't go off without some interference.'

A sister-in-law who was a potential thief—was that what he was thinking? But to admit that she had been using the driver's window as a mirror would provide him with further evidence of her vain and frivolous character—not part of her plan for the evening at all! Again, attack was the best defence, especially if it left him guessing.

She smiled. 'Nice stereo, isn't it? I'd get quite a bit for that from a bloke I know!'

His mouth twitched, but whether it was with disapproval or amusement she couldn't tell.

A heavy silence—Alex's rather than hers—followed, and, though he didn't seem disconcerted by it, she began to feel very uncomfortable as it lengthened. To break it, she said in tones less aggressive than she had at first planned, 'Rupert told me you had some business in Germany. When do you have to leave?'

He flicked a finger against his wine glass rim, and the expensive crystal gave out a sweet ringing sound.

'I've postponed it. Probably a couple of weeks.' *Weeks*! That was the worst thing she'd heard yet!

'Will you—will you be staying here at Derrham?' She hoped she wasn't betraying her dislike of the idea too obviously. This was developing into a strange sort of skirmish, and she wasn't sure how to proceed.

That dark blue gaze rested on her thoughtfully now. 'I don't know yet. Some of the time.'

Silence again. They were sitting at one end of a very long table, and irrelevantly it crossed her mind that if Alex had chosen one end of it, and Rupert the other, she'd have spent her time halfway between them, sliding the dishes up and down the table like a barman with the drinks in an old western.

Rather desperately, she changed the subject at random. In Alex's company a normal relaxed conversation seemed impossible. His contribution was either barbed or non-existent. 'This house must have a fascinating history— I asked Rupert about it, but he said you were the person who could tell me,' she suggested. At least the subject seemed innocuous.

'What did you want to know?' His manner wasn't encouraging, and his critical gaze rested on her face unwaveringly.

'Well—I...' She said the first thing that came into her head. 'This table—I was wondering how they got it in here. It's much too big to be turned in through the doors from the passage outside!'

Alex raised an eyebrow. 'It was built in here in Oliver Cromwell's time. All the house servants used to eat with the family in those days.'

'I was wondering about that too,' she said, pursuing the topic. His reply had been harmless enough. 'I thought the Tarrants must have gone in for an awful lot of children!'

The upward quirk to one side of his mouth acknowledged her attempt at humour. 'They did,' he agreed. 'But we seem to have let the side down recently. John Tarrant, who bought the house from a Royalist in the 1620s, had thirteen children. My father had only one.'

'So Rupert isn't your brother, then?'

'My half-brother. My mother married again after my father died. She's been widowed twice—Edward Stretton died a couple of years ago.'

He gave the answers in a way that left her no clue as to his feelings about any of the information he was offering. She tried a more personal aspect.

'Do you and your ex-wife have any children?' It was the first time it had occurred to her that he might be a father—which would make Rupert an uncle. The idea amused her. Her view of uncles was that they were staid, responsible and rather boring, like her own. A disapproving lift of the eyebrow reminded her that her knowledge of Vicky's existence couldn't have come from Alex himself, which implied that she must have been gossiping about him.

'A daughter.'

The tone was so cold and curt now; it was obvious that any other enquiries along that line would be most unwelcome. She studied him sideways, remembering his questions in the pub about her relationship with her own father. His expression was shuttered and withdrawn. Then his dark blue glance met hers.

'How are the lace handkerchiefs?' The slightly mocking amusement as he turned the subject to her own concerns, and the dismissive way in which he asked the question, annoyed her.

'Fine,' she said flippantly. 'I only do one in about three weeks. I find the work so exhausting.'

'That can't pay very much.'

'Oh, you'd be surprised. It's a highly specialised skill, mending Victorian lace. We don't make the same patterns now, you know, so each piece of work is different. I spend hours just staring at them. That's why I have to charge so much per handkerchief.'

He was looking at her quizzically. 'How much *do* you charge exactly?'

She didn't care what she said. It was frustrating to have had the subject changed just when she thought she might be getting somewhere. If he threw her out at the end of the evening, she'd get Rupert to give her a lift to the station and go home. She'd had enough of him.

'About three hundred pounds each. That of course covers the insurance.'

It was an outrageous figure, and it was the first time she heard Alex Tarrant laugh.

'So, Sophie, you live on an income of three hundred a month—or are you entirely a lady of leisure?'

It was a pity he didn't laugh more often. When his handsome face creased into laughter lines, she could see why other women would find him extremely attractive. 'Oh, I do a few other things to make ends meet.'

His amusement had completely disarmed her. She was unprepared for the barb in his next comment. 'You know Rupert isn't my heir, don't you? He doesn't have any money of his own.'

At first she didn't see the connection. Her finely arched brows drew together in a slight frown.

'Rupert . . . ?' Then she remembered she was supposed to be engaged to him. Alex saw her as a gold-digger! Outrage struggled with a certain satisfaction that he could have been taken in at all by the deception. She would have thought him far too astute.

'Oh, that doesn't matter to me,' she assured him scornfully. 'Rupert and I li-love each other for ourselves. After all, *nobody* marries a concert pianist for his money, do they?'

There was that downward, slightly sardonic turn to the corner of his mouth. 'Don't they, if they think he's inheriting a castle? So what do you intend to live on—air?'

She wasn't sure what line to take now. She wished desperately Rupert would come back. It was his fault she'd been drawn into a discussion of this kind in the first place. She tried to assess her position as his so-called fiancée: if she had been engaged to him, would it really be the right thing to enquire about his finances from his half-brother? Surely he would have told her himself. In her present circumstances, such an enquiry seemed in the worst possible taste. She assumed he must make some money from his concerts, but maybe what Alex was now telling her was that it was he who largely financed Rupert's career. Was he also saying that when she married him he wouldn't be able to count on the continuation of that financial support? Alex seemed to have quite a good relationship with his half-brother, but she wouldn't put it past him to cut off the money supply if he disapproved of his intended bride. Poor old Rupert!

She was determined now to keep the story of the engagement going for just as long as it took to show up Alex Tarrant for the unscrupulous man he was, but, to her intense relief, her 'fiancé' returned just then, which put a stop to the topic Alex had seen fit to explore. She needed time to think out a further strategy.

She was uncomfortably aware of him watching Rupert and herself through the rest of the meal, but although they put on a good show for his benefit, exchanging 'darling's with abandon, she couldn't help wondering if her earlier smug satisfaction had had any justification: there were times when Alex looked as though he didn't believe a word of the engagement.

Later they went into a small sitting-room, but when Rupert insisted on making the coffee, brushing aside all her offers of help, she was again left very unwillingly alone with Alex. The evening was becoming far more of an ordeal that she had bargained for! She wondered how early she could go to bed.

In order to avoid further discussion of the precise nature of her relationship with Rupert, she picked up the first book she could find and opened it. It turned out to be an old family photograph album. She glanced

across at her host, his tall figure propped with a rather
disconcerting masculine grace casually beside the fire-
place, one arm along the mantelpiece, one hand in his
trouser pocket. He was watching her.

'Do you mind if I look at this?' she asked.

'Go ahead,' he replied curtly. 'Past generations of
Tarrants—the official family record from my great-
grandfather's time onwards. Not particularly entertaining.'

She sat down with the book on her knee. It was very
heavy, and bound with leather. The last pages were still
blank, as though they awaited generations of Tarrants
yet to come. The oldest sepia-tinted photographs con-
sisted of many studio poses of the Tarrant uncles, aunts
and cousins with their first names written underneath;
then there were groups of servants on the castle steps,
the women in maids' uniforms, the men in waistcoats,
trousers and boots, some of them in livery. There were
family groups, and house parties out shooting, or round
the tennis net, and several young women dressed for
presentation at court in long white ball gowns of thirties
style, with Prince of Wales feathers in their hair. Sophie,
fascinated by the contrast in lifestyle with her own very
ordinary family snaps, turned her way slowly towards
the last pages, where she found a picture of an excep-
tionally good-looking young Guards officer, with
'Charles—1949' written underneath. The resemblance
to Alex was striking.

'Is this your father?' she asked, twisting the heavy
album on her knee so that he could see it more easily.
The looks of the young man in the photograph instantly
attracted her: it was easy to see that he must have had
great charm. That was a characteristic she would never
have conceded to Alex, except in an abstract way where
other women were concerned. But in spite of her dismissive judgement of him, she was aware again of the
extraordinarily powerful effect he had on her as he came

to stand beside her. It was disconcerting that the effect
didn't diminish as she got to know him better—if anything, the opposite seemed to be happening. It was as
though her body registered its impressions of him entirely independently of her mind. Balancing the book on
her knees, she put her hands in her lap. It was ridiculous, but she was afraid they might shake.

'That was taken just after he married my mother,' Alex
said in answer to her question, speaking just behind her,
and the deep, mellow voice almost literally sent shivers
down her spine. He turned a page. 'That's my mother.'

At first, in a sort of blur, she was aware only of his
hand, holding the page, the well-shaped sensitive fingers
and the fine gold signet ring.

'Is that the crest of the Tarrants?' she asked irrelevantly. Her mind was playing tricks with her again; for
one awful moment all she could think of was what it
must be like to feel the touch of that hand in a caress...

'One of them,' he was saying. 'There's more than one
branch of this particular family.'

In an attempt to break free of the disconcerting spell
that seemed to possess her, she resorted to the old antagonism, grasping the first thing that came to mind,
and found herself slightly irritated—how very feudal it
all seemed! If that was the way Alex really ticked, he
should have been living in another age—no wonder he
didn't think her good enough even for his younger
brother!

She ignored the niggling suspicion that she was doing
him an injustice; he was beginning to evoke too many
complicated reactions in her, and it was easier to dislike
him. She turned her attention to the album again.

The woman in the photograph couldn't have been
more than eighteen. She was strikingly beautiful. There
was no doubt of her relationship either to Alex, or to
Rupert. They both had her classic perfection of features
and dark hair.

She didn't pass a comment. His tone hadn't invited one. He continued to stand beside her as she turned over the last two pages. There were photographs of children—two boys. It was easy to recognise Alex, and the very much younger Rupert.

The last page had several ragged gaps, where pictures had been torn out.

'What happened to these?' It was curious that anyone should feel strongly enough about photographs to go to the trouble of tearing them out of a family album like that.

She was surprised at the sudden bitterness in his reply. 'My ex-wife. One was a wedding photograph, and there were a couple of portraits of her and Louisa—our daughter.'

'But why did she tear them out?'

He sounded impatient. 'A way of making the point that she no longer wanted to be associated with the Tarrant family?'

Once again, his tone warned her off any further comment, and before she could indulge any unwise curiosity Rupert came in with the coffee.

She went to bed that night feeling she had definitely passed through an ordeal, but with modified views of her host. She didn't like him any better—after all, his attitude to her continued to be extremely unflattering—but she was prepared to allow that he might be more complex a character than he had at first appeared. He sounded as though he was still very bitter about his ex-wife. Then she reminded herself that Vicky, whatever she was like, might have had very good reason for wanting to shake off the Tarrants. Alex Tarrant hadn't called to mind the image of a saint at their first meeting. Quite the opposite!

But any sympathy she might have been tempted to feel in that direction was firmly crushed the following morning. She was passing the library on her way to breakfast when she heard the sound of piano keys, and stopped with the intention of finding out if Rupert was going to join her. Then she heard Alex's voice, and it became obvious that the pianist was merely amusing himself in the middle of some discussion.

Alex's voice was unmistakable. 'Don't take me for a fool, Rupert. I've watched the two of you together. You're putting on an act for each other.'

His brother's voice in reply sounded light but firm. 'And don't you confuse her with Vicky. She's a very different sort of person. You're not being fair to her!'

She could hear Alex's snort of contempt. 'So far I haven't seen any evidence that she isn't just as empty-headed and self-seeking. She isn't in love with you. And I'm not convinced that you're in love with her. Whatever you're up to, I wish you'd go and do it somewhere else.'

Rupert sounded slightly defensive now. 'You've always told me I can invite whoever I like to Derrham. Why make an exception of Sophie? She isn't going to steal the silver—she's perfectly civilised!'

'That's not the point, and you know it.'

There was a ripple of arpeggios up and down the piano before Rupert spoke. 'I happen to think Sophie's wonderful. She's going to marry me, and she's staying!'

Mortified, her face burning, she made her way stiffly to the kitchen. She'd heard more than enough. 'Empty-headed and self-seeking'—just like Vicky! His judgement of her was humiliating in the extreme.

It was galling too to learn that, although Alex's hospitality might extend unquestioningly to any of Rupert's other friends, an exception was being made in her case. She had no intention of marrying Rupert, so his step-brother's opinions on that particular matter should be irrelevant to her, but it didn't do much for her self-esteem to learn that, had the engagement been a genuine one, she would have been an unacceptable choice. Surely the feudal attitudes she had attributed to him earlier couldn't

really underlie his objection to her? Had he formed his
impressions of her purely on the basis of one recording
session during which she featured in the most menial
capacity of all?

Rupert had said, 'Don't you confuse her with Vicky...'
She must remind Alex very strongly indeed of his former
wife. His replies about the photograph album had been
tinged with great bitterness, and he had shut off all
further lines of question about his daughter. Then the
act of tearing out the photographs seemed an over-
dramatic gesture, provoked by great anger, or resentment, on Vicky's part. They must have split up on
very bad terms. Perhaps he now hated her and, so far,
there had been no indications about the house that Alex
had ever had a wife or a child; their traces were obliter-
ated, as though they had never been.

She did toy with the idea of confessing to Alex that
the engagement had been no more than a silly joke. He
would think it pretty pointless, but his objections to her
might be less in evidence, and a more congenial time
could be had by all. But when she thought about it
further she decided it wouldn't make much difference.
It wouldn't alter *her* attitude to *him*. He didn't think she
was good enough for the Tarrants. But so what? He
wasn't nearly good enough for the Carters... No, she
wouldn't tell him! She'd just let him stew while he believed that she was going to be Mrs Rupert Stretton. Then
she'd break off the 'engagement' in a few weeks' time
on the grounds that her family didn't approve of his
brother.

In her new decisive mode, geared for instant departure, she left her coffee unfinished and ran upstairs
to consult the train timetable she'd left on her dressing-
table. It made her feel a lot better. She didn't have to
stay, especially now her real host had made it clear she
was not welcome.

Rupert came upstairs after a while and found her in the middle of packing, her clothes spread all over the bed.

'What on earth are you doing?' he demanded at once. 'You can't go! Is this because of Alex?'

She folded a jersey with aggressive determination. She wasn't going to show that underneath she was hurt by the whole episode. 'I overheard your conversation a while ago in the library. I didn't want to listen, but I couldn't miss the way Alex was voicing his objections!'

'Hey—cool down!' Rupert threw himself into her bedroom chair with the kind of graceful ease that made her think unwillingly of Alex. 'What does his opinion of you matter? You're not going to marry me anyway!' Somehow that was as hurtful as anything Alex had said— as though her feelings were only valid if she were genu- inely engaged to Rupert, and being rejected for herself didn't matter! The Strettons were every bit as bad as the Tarrants.

'Well, thank you very much, Rupert!' she exclaimed crossly. 'You've got the same line in flattery as your de- lightful brother—though not quite his inimitable sting, I'll grant you!'

To her surprise, he looked rather shamefaced all of a sudden. 'Sorry, Sophe. It's not fair to you really. He's always interfering in my life—vetting my girlfriends, that sort of thing. I couldn't resist trying to stop him in his tracks just for once. I suppose he's only trying to save me from a disastrous marriage.'

She ignored the insult implicit in that—he obviously hadn't realised it was there. 'So is this the way he be- haves towards every woman who reminds him of Vicky?'

Rupert shrugged. 'Oh, don't pay any attention to it. He's just never quite got her out of his system.'

That seemed like a pretty feeble reason to her. Surely it couldn't account for *all* his animosity? There had to be more to it than that!

But Rupert was still explaining. 'She won't let him see Louisa, his daughter, even though he's got rights to her. He tried to get full custody of her, but there was the usual bias in favour of the mother. Alex was very cut up about it.'

That altered the picture of her host a little, but it didn't really mend matters, and it took all Rupert's persuasive powers to get her to reconsider.

'So when is he going?' she demanded finally.

'I'm not sure exactly. He's just giving this German recording company a chance to sort itself out. It could be no more than a couple of days. Please stay!' Her resentment cooled a little. If there was a possibility Alex really would be gone in two days, it would be a pity to cut short her holiday unnecessarily. But if *he* didn't leave after that, *she* would. 'All right,' she agreed slowly. 'But if he has one more go at me—just one more!—I'm catching the next train to London. I mean it, Rupert!'

Later that day Rupert went out to try the piano on which he was to give a recital. Alex had been safely out of the way since the morning; according to his brother, he had gone to visit one of his tenants, and in his absence she preferred to stay at Derrham. She had intended to spend some of the day working on a small nineteenth-century sampler a friend had asked her to mend, and was looking forward to a few undisturbed hours in the library, her favourite room, in the peace and quiet of the house she was beginning to love despite its hostile owner.

She established herself in a comfortable chair by a window with a good view of the drive, in case Alex came back suddenly. Mrs Bates came in once, to replace an old arrangement of flowers, apologising for her intrusion.

'That's all right,' Sophie said brightly. 'Do you do all the flowers in the house, Mrs Bates? They're really wonderful.'

The compliment was well deserved, and she was pleased to see the other woman beam with pleasure. She liked Ellen Bates, and had had several conversations with her in the kitchen before Alex's arrival, but if she had any complaint about the cook-housekeeper it was that she was infuriatingly discreet about her employer! She suspected Ellen might be prepared to take a few minutes off for a chat, judging from the ineffectual way she was flicking her duster, and encouraged her to talk about the old days at Derrham. Privately she was hoping for more information about its present owner, but the picture Ellen drew was that of any great house declining from its former glory.

'So what about when Mr Tarrant's wife lived here...?' Sophie pursued. 'Were there many more people employed then?'

Ellen pursed her lips thoughtfully. 'Well, things were beginning to wind down a bit then, you might say. When Mr Tarrant first married—he was very young then, only twenty-two—his father was still alive, though Mr Alex was taking over the running of the estate.'

'And his wife...? I haven't seen any pictures of her anywhere, though I'm not really surprised. What did she look like?'

Her hopes of leading the housekeeper on to speak more freely were disappointed. All too quickly, 'discretion' was written over Ellen's face in large letters.

'A bit like you, I'd say,' she offered cautiously. 'My, look at the time! I'd better get on or there'll be no lunch!'

She had whisked the old arrangement off the table and was through the door before Sophie could get in another word.

She took a break from the sampler-mending later to try out the piano. In a pile of books on a library shelf, she found some simple music in a child's collection of nursery rhymes. On the cover were the words: 'To Louisa Mary Tarrant' in handwriting she recognised as Rupert's, and underneath it the name had been repeated in a childish scrawl.

At least she knew the tunes. She began to amuse herself with them, quickly becoming engrossed, leaning over the piano, her expression absorbed, as she picked out the notes. She was unaware that the library door had opened, and that she was being watched.

When she looked up suddenly, it was a shock to see Alex standing there, a dark frown on his face. She gave a gasp, her brown eyes wide, and put her hand on her chest in a gesture of fright. 'You scared me—I didn't know you were here!'

'Where did you find that book?'

His question wasn't exactly hostile, but instantly she was on the defensive. She couldn't forget that in this man's eyes she was just a second-rate citizen—not good enough to join the family ranks.

'Here, on the shelves,' she said with a certain amount of defiance. 'Should I have asked your permission or something?' Her tone made it quite clear that she would have regarded any such requirement as unacceptable.

He shrugged. 'No. Take what books you like. I didn't know you could read music.'

So they were back to that again!

'Only when Rupert's written the letters of the notes on the keys for me,' she said sweetly. That might give him a bad moment—she couldn't imagine him taking kindly to anyone pencilling on the ivory of his Steinway grand.

He took a stride into the room. 'Where is Rupert?'

'Gone to try out a piano.'

He acknowledged her reply with a curt nod. Then the sampler, which she had left on top of the piano lid, caught his eye. 'Getting on with the hankies, are you?'

She felt like sticking her tongue out at him. 'That's a doll's tablecloth.'

Her earlier decision to leave—only conditionally reversed—refuelled her spirit. She felt they were skating again, speeding over the ice, and this time it was very thin indeed.

He gave her another of his quizzical looks, then remarked casually, 'Rupert tells me you mend tapestries in your spare time.'

'When I can fit one in between the hankies, yes.' She returned his look with a hostile stare.

'What do you think of the one on the stairs?'

'Flemish. Seventeenth-century,' she said shortly. 'It needs mending.'

He gave her a long, considering look. 'Could you do it?'

Work! *The Successful Businesswoman* advised—'never miss an opportunity', although she had the feeling that somehow this one disguised an oblique attack. She wouldn't commit herself to anything yet—not when it involved Alex.

'I'd have to have a good look at it,' she said carefully.

'Would you like to give me your opinion on it now?' The request was politely phrased, but as always, despite the mellow tones, he had a way of making it sound like a command.

Her instinctive reaction was to say 'No!', but professional pride came to her rescue. He could merely be making use of her for a free consultation, but he might also be prepared to offer her the job. If he did, it would be hard to refuse—but she would insist on taking the tapestry away with her, despite the difficulties involved. There was no way she would stay on as an unwelcome guest in his house.

With a shrug, she got up from the piano. 'OK,' she agreed ungraciously.

She followed his tall figure into the hall and halfway up the staircase. The tapestry hung, a glowing mural, against the dark panelling. If he asked her to repair it, it would be the biggest she'd ever done. It was difficult to see more than about a third in any detail, and she went further up the stairs to get a better view. The threads were very worn; in places the fabric had been attacked by moth. One whole section had been inexpertly stitched by someone in the past, and the tear was still obvious. It would have to be redone.

Alex remained on the stairs while she went up to the landing without a word, and leaned over the carved wooden banister for a closer inspection. He was looking up at her, not at the hanging. She would have preferred to be left alone; while he was there below her she found it difficult to concentrate, too acutely conscious of his attention.

The top of the tapestry was still some way above her, and poorly lit. It looked as though the upper border would need a reconstruction job, but she couldn't be sure.

'Is there a light switch?' She looked at him.

'On the wall behind you.'

An immense chandelier hung in the stairwell, decked with sparkling glass like waterdrops on a spider's web—beautiful, and no doubt extremely valuable, but useless. The top border remained obscure in the gloom. She glanced down at Alex again. 'I still can't see it properly. Your ancestral lighting's all very well as an ornament, but it's not much practical use, is it?'

She saw the line of his jaw tighten suddenly. Then he said, 'You sound like my ex-wife. She didn't have much time for the family valuables either, except as quick access to cash.'

The meaning he had extracted from her remark was so far from the intention behind it that she felt insulted. His implication—that she only saw old and beautiful things from a commercial point of view—was hurtful, although it revealed something of his attitude towards Vicky. But it was an increasing irritation to be seen all the time in terms of someone else—someone she'd never met and suspected she wouldn't like if she did.

She bit back the reply she was tempted to make, and headed for the stairs again, to examine more closely the part of the tapestry she could actually reach. As she expected, it had been stitched to a backing which would have to be reinforced. It was probably holding the whole thing together.

She stood for a while assessing it. Alex remained where he was, only a few steps below her now, watching her. At last he said, 'What's your estimate, then?'

She looked down at him, and without hesitation named a price well into four figures. The expression of scepticism that instantly crossed his face riled her more than his words.

'Don't you think that's a bit steep?'

Most people were surprised when she quoted a price for restoration, but their expression was usually one of dismay, not disbelief. But in Alex's case his objection could scarcely have been prompted by money problems. He was doubting her professional competence. He must be able to see that to repair a tapestry of that size was a considerable undertaking: there was the cost of the materials involved, the difficulty in finding specially dyed wools to match the old faded ones, and the amount of time it took to repair even one small section. To do it badly would be to ruin it. He obviously didn't think her work could be worth the amount she was charging for it. He had a way of undervaluing her as a person that cut away at her whole identity.

'No,' she said, her brown eyes suddenly burning with a mixture of intense feelings she didn't want to analyse. 'I think it's cheap! I should have asked more. I can't quote a firm price unless I examine the whole thing properly, but, on second thoughts, I'd probably add another fifteen hundred to the figure I've just given you!'

He was silent. Then he said, 'How do I know you could do this? Do I know anyone you've done any work for?'

She was seething—from anyone else the query would have been reasonable, though it might have been phrased more tactfully, but from him, in the context of his earlier remarks and his general attitude, she couldn't accept it.

'I'll send you a complete list of the London museums I've done any work for, shall I?' she demanded angrily. 'Oh, and the names, addresses and private telephone numbers of the clients who've seen fit to trust me with their family heirlooms.'

Her voice shook, and she didn't dare go on. Even without the aid of *The Successful Businesswoman* she'd learned that a certain amount of bluff was necessary— but her museum work to date hadn't strictly been within the London boundary, and the heirlooms had been very minor indeed in comparison with the one he could offer!

She turned abruptly and awkwardly on the stairs, intending to take refuge in her bedroom—anywhere to get away from him before he either discovered the precise nature of her past experience, or provoked her to tell him exactly what she thought of him and obliged her to walk out before he threw her out. But as she turned, her foot caught the edge of the step beneath her, and momentarily she lost her balance. His reaction was instantaneous. He caught hold of her by the arm to steady her, and the unexpected contact swung her against him. As she came up against the solid wall of his chest, she was almost in his arms.

The moment of contact froze her with shock...and suddenly it was as though she had fallen on the same side of the fence as a lion she had been teasing—or a dangerous tiger. Between their highly charged encounters there had always been a safety barrier, but now, without warning, it had vanished.

She was totally unprepared for the extraordinary effect of the contact on her body. Something seemed to surge through her—a fire, or a flood—that swept all her normal rational reactions before it, filling her with a new and delicious sensation of weakness that was entirely strange to her. If he had not been gripping her by the upper arms, she would have fallen. As it was, she was almost lying against his chest. She found herself staring up into those contemptuous blue eyes—and experienced a further shock. Instead of the gleam of dislike she might have expected to find there, they were surprisingly dark, and their expression baffled her. For one completely irrational moment she thought he was going to kiss her.

But even as their eyes met, he released her—so abruptly that she stumbled back on to the step above her. At that moment there was the electronic shrilling of a telephone, and before she had time to gather her wits, or regain her balance, Alex had turned on his heel and was halfway down the stairs, two at a time.

She sat down hard, her eyes filling with tears as the base of her spine came into contact with the edge of the step. But they were more than tears of pain. She was smarting under the humiliating suspicion that, quite apart from the urgency of the summons, he had been only too anxious to get away from a physical contact with her that was both unexpected . . . and unwelcome.

CHAPTER FOUR

IT WASN'T easy to slam an old oak door with an ill-fitting latch, but Sophie did her best. Then, for the second time that day, she made straight for her suitcase and flung it on the bed. Somewhere in the struggling confusion of emotions he succeeded in arousing in her was the humiliating conviction that Alex Tarrant had now rejected her in every way possible. It wasn't that she had *wanted* him to kiss her—very far from it! But he needn't have made it quite so obvious that she was unattractive to him physically, as well as on all the other social and intellectual counts she seemed to have notched up.

No one had ever made her feel as he did—as though nothing she could have to offer was of any value at all! He had assessed her on sight as not being worth the trouble of engaging in serious conversation, and even when he discovered she had specialised skills he could make use of he had dismissed those too, by making it clear he thought she was over-pricing them.

With her open, affectionate nature, she'd never encountered anyone who had actively disliked her before, or caused her to doubt herself in any serious way. But Alex's arrogance and his coolly contemptuous manner were beginning to undermine all the things she had never questioned about herself. Well, there was no reason why she should go on staying under the same roof as him. From anyone else, a restoration job like the one he could offer her would be like manna from heaven at the moment. But there was no way she would endure any further contact with him—even if it was no closer than the end of a fax machine.

She was paying no attention to the way she was packing, flinging one garment into her suitcase after another. She decided to wear her linen jacket, and pack her light summer raincoat—it would mean fewer separate items to carry. Then she stuck a handful of pins in her hair. It was looking rather straggly since she had put it up that morning.

Still in a turmoil of emotions, she went out to reconnoitre. If Rupert returned in time, she'd make him give her a lift to the station on the grounds that she'd had an urgent phone call from her father. Alex would probably know there'd been no calls, but she didn't care what he thought now. He was the one who ought to be ashamed that he'd harassed one of his guests until she'd been forced to leave by the first available train.

Rupert had not yet returned. That meant an expensive taxi, but the situation could be classed as an emergency. She made her way to the kitchen to consult Ellen Bates. The back door was open, and just at that moment the housekeeper appeared with a bundle of washing in her arms.

'Looks like rain,' she commented. 'Just when we was having such a nice August, too.'

The urgency of the situation didn't allow much time for general chat, so, having established that Alex wouldn't be back for a couple of hours—good—and that Rupert had not yet returned—bad—conscience-stricken at the lie, she explained about the crisis at home, and her need to get to the station. It made her feel worse that Ellen looked genuinely concerned and went out instantly in search of Sam.

She was back in seconds. 'He says if you can be ready to leave now, he'll take you to Hereford, if you don't mind him doing a few errands first. Do you think you could leave straight away?'

Could she? Impulsively she gave the housekeeper a hug. 'You're a darling! I'll be down in two ticks!'

A few heavy drops of rain turned into a sudden downpour as she and Sam Bates, in the old Land Rover, followed a roundabout route through the lanes that took them up to a couple of farms, but she was relieved to see that it had eased off again by the time they reached Hereford station.

'Sorry I can't wait to see you catch your train all right,' Sam apologised. 'But I'd best be off straight away if I'm to get back to Derrham in time for Mr Alex. It wouldn't do to keep him waiting!'

'No—I don't suppose it would!' Privately she thought it might do him a lot of good, but it wasn't a remark it would be fair to make to the faithful Sam. She gave him a brilliant smile. 'Sam—thank you *very* much for the lift!'

'Pleasure!' He touched his cap in an old-fashioned gesture, and climbed back into the Land Rover. She experienced an unexpected twinge of regret as she watched the tail-gate disappear—it seemed like a last link with all that she loved about Derrham. But then, with a sudden vivid image of its owner in her mind, she turned resolutely back towards the station entrance.

It wasn't until she opened her handbag to check her ticket that she remembered: she had left it, together with all her money and her credit cards, on the dressing-table in her bedroom! She had been looking for some stamps that had fallen to the bottom of the bag, and had had to take everything out in her search. In her hasty departure, she'd forgotten all about the little pile of things on the dressing-table. She felt like cursing, crying and screaming all at once. What on earth was she going to do now? She didn't even have any change in her pocket for a telephone call.

A quick survey of the station forecourt showed her that there was not a taxi in sight. If she could get one soon enough, she could go back to Derrham to retrieve her money and ticket, and pay the driver on her return

to Hereford. But solving one problem could pose
another: Sam Bates's roundabout route to the station
had been time-consuming, and Alex might have already
returned—in which case it would be very difficult to
avoid a meeting with him. Even if she tried ringing
Rupert and reversing the charges, she might get Alex
instead . . .

She went to the ticket office.

'Do you know how long it might be before another
taxi comes along?' It was a stupid question, but you
never knew—perhaps the ticket office man's brother was
a taxi driver or something.

'Couldn't say. Where was you trying to get to?' There
was a woman behind her now, waiting to buy a ticket.
She felt very silly. Perhaps she should just ask directions
for Derrham from someone and then hitch. She would
have to ask to leave her bag—she couldn't carry that all
the way back to the castle.

She explained about Derrham, and about her money
and ticket, and just as she was going to ask about buses
the woman behind her said, 'I'll give you a lift! I can't
take you right down to Derrham, but I'll drop you a
couple of miles away if that's any good.'

Sophie turned round. The woman was somehow familiar. . . Then she remembered her wait for Rupert at
Leominster, and the station wagon that had drawn up
in front of the furniture restorer's. The woman, possibly
in her sixties, was wearing a headscarf and green water-
proof jacket, but if she'd suddenly sprouted wings and
a halo Sophie couldn't have felt more convinced that
heaven had intervened to save her.

The woman waved her gratitude aside. Within moments she had dealt satisfactorily with the matter of
leaving Sophie's suitcase for collection later, and entered
into a lengthy interrogation of her own over the price
of a ticket to Oxford for her granddaughter. Every sort
of ticket was discussed at length, and Sophie glanced

nervously at the clock as the minutes ticked past. Alex would be back at the castle by the time she returned if they didn't hurry, and her second departure would be a great deal more embarrassing than the first.

At last they made their way to the battered estate car, complete with dogs no less hysterical than before. She was relieved to see that they were cooped up behind a wire mesh this time. Her unknown driver took the bends unnervingly fast, swinging dogs and passenger from one side to the other as she negotiated the country lanes. To hold any sort of conversation above the noise of the car, it was necessary to shout.

'So you've been staying with Alex, have you?' the woman asked, without preamble, as soon as they had turned out of the station. She seemed to be well acquainted with the Tarrant family.

'Well, with Rupert actually.'

'Hmph. Ever met Alex's wife Vicky?'

What an odd question! 'No—I——'

'Never got on with her. Too calculating for my liking, and too frivolous for someone like Alex, though he was besotted with her when they first met. Married too young, of course. Never a success. Charming boy, Alex, but a bit too soft-hearted for his own good. How is he these days? Always very busy. Known him for years. And Rupert. Those dawgs all right?'

Alex—soft-hearted? But dutifully she turned to examine the setters. They were in a tumbled heap behind their wire.

'Fine—they——'

'So you're going to London?'

'Well, yes, I have to go home to see my father,' she said quickly, hoping to dispose of the story before her rescuer could ask too many disconcerting questions, only to pass on some inconvenient detail to Alex in a chance conversation. 'Mr Bates gave me a lift to the station, but we left in a hurry and I forgot my ticket.'

'Good man, Bates,' said her companion decidedly. 'Been trying to get him to work for me for years, but there's no tempting him away from the Tarrants. Alex's like his father in that—always good to his staff.'

Sophie thought about that comment while a long, very general monologue followed on the virtues of a good gardener. She wondered whether Alex paid well, or whether the remark meant that he handed out lord-of-the-manor-type gifts at Christmas, and ground the faces of the poor the rest of the time. It was what she was tempted to think of him, but the evidence seemed otherwise. The Bates couple were obviously devoted to him.

And then there was that other remark—'too soft-hearted for his own good'! Alex was the last person in the world to whom she would apply a comment like that! There seemed nothing soft about him at all. Perhaps it was a side of him that had been reserved for Vicky and his daughter. According to Rupert, he had been upset that Vicky had denied him access to Louisa. Alex the father—that was an aspect of him she couldn't imagine at all.

Suddenly they were pulling up beside a gate into a field, allowing her just enough room to open the passenger door.

'Sorry I can't take you all the way down to Derrham,' her rescuer announced, 'but I turn off here. Straight along this road to the next signpost, and then turn to your right. My love to Alex when you see him. Must get on—shut up, dawgs!'

Sophie scarcely had time to shout her thanks over the chorus of barking before she found herself standing in the lane, watching the station wagon swing wildly round a bend, the three manic animals crammed against the back window.

The lanes were now muddy from the recent rain, and the sky unremittingly grey overhead. Her raincoat was still in her suitcase at the station and she wished now she'd worn sensible shoes; high heels were for city streets, not for the country. But if she could just reach Derrham before the threatened cloudburst, she felt she could cope with anything she might have to deal with once there.

She felt intensely annoyed with herself and life in general. Just her luck to find herself tottering back to the very house she'd managed to leave so easily! Her chances of meeting Alex when she got back increased with every passing minute. Drops of rain began to fall.

She almost had to jump into the ditch as an oncoming car swung round the corner towards her a little too fast, and then a van sprayed her with muddy water from a puddle. She felt crosser than ever with life, and bedraggled into the bargain. Her linen jacket would soon be clinging to her, and her hair would be hanging in rats' tails.

When she heard another vehicle approaching from behind she was almost ready to shake her fist at the driver. There was a farm gate just a few paces ahead, and she quickened her step in order to reach it before the car repeated the spraying trick. She glanced back once to see a dark blue Jaguar approaching, and then stepped quickly on to the wet grass verge to let it pass safely, her high heels embedding themselves in the mud.

To her surprise, the driver pulled up a little way ahead of her, and then began to reverse. The car was unfamiliar to her. All sorts of gruesome newspaper headlines flashed through her mind, and she had visions of herself lying murdered in the ditch.

The car stopped beside her, and the door on the driver's side opened. A split second before he got out, she knew who it was. Her heart gave an ominous thud. Why on earth couldn't it have been Rupert? She was only too conscious of her last interview with his brother on the stairs. Wild ideas of escape flitted through her head, but, since most of them involved clearing a five-foot hedge from a standing jump, she had to abandon them as impractical. Then she found herself staring across the car roof into those critical blue eyes, now all too familiar.

'Sophie!'

Did he sound faintly surprised, or was it a demand for an explanation? The rain was beginning to fall more heavily now. Even the weather was against her.

'Going for a walk?'

'Yes,' she said defiantly. And then regretted it. High heels and a conspicuous absence of umbrella. It would have been much simpler to have stuck to her phone-call-from-home story.

'Want a lift?'

'No, thank you.' She answered on impulse, resenting the way in which all the advantages invariably seemed to range themselves on his side.

The sceptical gaze took in her rain-soaked linen jacket liberally speckled with mud, and bedraggled ends of hair, now dripping in an artistic manner into her collar. Then his eyes rested uncompromisingly on her face again, and she could see amusement lurking somewhere in their blue depths, which made her crosser and more uncomfortable than ever.

'You enjoy getting wet in the rain?' he asked, in tones that left her in no doubt that that was the last thing he believed of her.

She could feel herself blushing as he waited for her to resort to an explanation. She gave in.

'I—er—had to ring my father while you were out. He seemed quite keen I should come home as there's a sort of . . . well, minor family crisis . . .'

She began to tail off. It was difficult to tell a pack of lies when the look in somebody's eyes told you they didn't believe a word of it.

'London's that direction.' With a casual flick of the finger, he indicated the way she had come.

Taking heart from the thought that the next bit anyway was true, she began on the saga of the train ticket, before faltering to a halt for the second time. 'I left my suitcase at the station... And by the way, the woman with the dogs sent her love to you... I forgot to ask what her name was.'

'Betty Laitham. It's her recital you're supposed to be going to with Rupert. Weren't you page turning for him?' He made it sound as though she had changed her mind on a whim, and would be letting Rupert down.

'I thought *you* might like to do that—you're obviously better at it than me!' she shot back. His earlier insults on the subject still rankled.

Raindrops were falling faster all the time, and it looked as though the lowering summer clouds had now decided to spill their entire contents on the lanes and fields immediately surrounding Derrham.

'You've still got a couple of miles to go,' Alex pointed out heartlessly, 'and I'm not standing about chatting in a downpour just for fun.' There was a loaded pause. 'Get in.'

Her immediate reaction was, as always, rebellious. If he'd asked her rather than told her, she might have felt more like accepting the lift which it would be only common sense to take—within minutes she'd look like a drowned rat, and then there'd be an uncomfortable wait once she finally got back to the station, followed by the long journey home. She could have pneumonia by the time she got to London! If her age and cast of character had allowed it, she would have burst there and then into childish and stormy tears. But, in the circumstances, her reluctance to go anywhere in the company of her least favourite man was outweighed by the prospect of a long, cold, wet walk. As a dismal little trickle edged down her neck and investigated her collarbone, she found her decision already made.

'OK,' she said ungraciously, and opened the car door.

If there had been spikes in her seat, and a battery of weapons between the two of them, all pointing in her direction, she couldn't have felt more uncomfortable or wary. He was only inches away from her, and for all of two miles she was trapped.

She would have liked to sit in silence for the rest of the journey—it would have avoided the necessity of discussing further her reasons for leaving, and there would have been no opportunity to get into a difficult conversation. But Alex asked immediately, 'What sort of a family crisis is this?' He gave her a sideways glance. 'Serious?'

'No, no. Nothing dreadful,' she said with finality, hoping he wouldn't pursue the topic.

'But you're needed back at home.'

'Yes.'

Silence again. He was obviously waiting for her to fill in a few more details. Reluctantly she said, 'It's—it's my aunt. She—er—had a slight accident, and my father wanted me at home to look after her house.'

'I see.' She couldn't guess from those deep, even tones whether he believed her or not, but then he said, 'You haven't just walked out in a fit of pique because of something that happened earlier?'

He was too astute. The aunt story would need a lot more conviction if he was going to swallow it! But what exactly was he alluding to—their barbed exchange over the chandelier, or the annoyance she had shown at his doubts about her professional competence? Or was it a hint that he suspected the true cause of her departure: the abrupt manner in which he had left her to answer the phone when she had almost fallen into his arms? But she was aware that any explanation of her real objection would be impossible to give, since it was something far more subtle and insulting than his merely abandoning her in answer to an urgent summons; his rejection of her had been on a personal level—it had had nothing to do with a telephone call.

It seemed unwise to commit herself too far in her reply, but before she could say anything he asked, 'You haven't had a row with Rupert?'

'With *Rupert*?'

Her surprise gave it away.

'Do I gather from that that you think you've had a row with somebody else?' He waited just a fraction of a second. 'Me, perhaps?'

'I don't know what you mean!' It was a feeble defence, but it was all she could do not to gasp.

She could have hated him when he began to laugh with genuine amusement. 'How old are you, Sophie?'

'Too old to have to answer that question!' she said waspishly, certain that there was a criticism lurking somewhere behind it. 'Are you implying that I look older or I act younger?'

'As you've set it up so that I insult you both ways, I decline to reply.' He still looked very entertained, and his more relaxed manner did nothing to ease the tension that for her seemed to underlie every exchange. He glanced at her again. 'It's a pity you've decided to go. I've been thinking about our discussion this morning— I've got a proposition to put to you.'

'Oh?' It wasn't difficult to sound dismissive of it. After all, could *any* proposition from a man like Alex Tarrant be welcome to her?

'The tapestry on the stairs. I don't think the price you quoted was unreasonable.'

'Check up on it, did you?' she demanded, pertly. The side of his mouth twitched—a sign that he was still amused, or merely trying to keep his temper?

'Since you ask—I have friends in the business.' Rival restorers? She had a moment of doubt then, even though she'd told herself she wasn't interested—he could ask someone else to do the job and then she'd miss her chance.

'I spoke to a friend who deals in antiques,' Alex was saying. 'He gave me some idea of what it might cost to get something of that size repaired.'

'Which price are we talking about?' she asked shrewdly. 'My first quote, or my revised estimate?'

Unexpectedly, he smiled. 'The revised one! Been doing a bit of homework?'

'What do you mean?'

'*The Successful Businesswoman* . . . You left it on a table in the library. So how is business?'

'Fine!' she said in hard, bright tones.

'Then you'd be too busy to do any work for me?'

'I'm going back to London.'

'So you are.'

Another silence, while she wondered if she'd just bluffed her way out of a worthwhile job, and thought about how much she needed the money. And how much, if it were for anyone but Alex, she would enjoy doing the restoration of such a beautiful piece. She could have taken a smaller tapestry safely away, but the stair hanging at Derrham was too unwieldy. She would have to have a frame on to which it could be rolled. That would have to be made specially; she had nothing wide enough. But that was no problem—a friend of her father's had made frames to her specifications before. Then the cleaning would have to be done before she started on the restoration. She could use some of that time to contact her supplier to match the wools. Within a couple of weeks Alex would surely be gone, and that was the minimum time needed to sort out the cleaning and have the frame built. The real drawback was having to stay at Derrham at all . . . Then she realised she was more than halfway to accepting his offer!

There was another brief silence.

'You wouldn't consider coming back to have a look at the tapestry once your aunt's crisis is sorted out?' He was surprisingly persistent, and she hesitated openly this time. The money was very tempting. With no other immediate prospects of a sum like that, she'd be a fool to turn him down on purely personal grounds.

'What do you normally do—take the tapestry away with you?' he asked.

'If it isn't too big, yes.'

'Then you'd have to stay at Derrham while you worked on it. Think about it.'

His words might have been meant purely as encouragement, but as usual they sounded like an order, and instantly her hackles rose. However, she bit back the negative retort she was about to give; it wasn't the time to antagonise him again if she wanted to keep her options open. She couldn't tell what he was thinking. The calm classic profile gave nothing away.

'I didn't recognise your car,' she began in a bid to change the topic, and then asked pointedly, 'Has somebody stolen the other one?'

He didn't react to that. Perhaps he had forgotten about the alarm episode. 'The Porsche doesn't like country lanes. This is more comfortable to drive.'

There was another silence, but his mood still seemed more congenial than before and it was hard to keep up the same level of resentment, though she didn't give it up easily.

'So you have a vehicle for every type of road?'

He ignored the sarcasm in her tone. 'No, but you're welcome to borrow a car while you're staying—assuming you've got a driving licence?'

'I'm on my way home,' she pointed out shortly.

'Of course.'

She considered next his unexpected offer of a car. What was it—an extra incentive to get her to stay, now that he found he could get the tapestry repaired at a bargain price? But it was possible, taking into account the opinions of Betty Laitham and Ellen, that she was doing him an injustice.

'I'm sorry I have to leave so suddenly,' she began as a sop to common politeness, just in case, unlikely though it seemed, he had been inspired by genuine kindness. 'I was—I was going to write to thank you for having me to stay. I wasn't sure when you or Rupert would be back, and I couldn't wait around to explain.'

'So Rupert doesn't know you're intending to go back to London?'

'Well, not when I left. No. I suppose he might by now, if he's back at home.'

Alex raised one dark eyebrow at that, but he made no further comment.

There was no sign of Rupert, however, when they arrived at Derrham, though they were very quickly met by Mrs Bates, who appeared round the side of the house as soon as Alex's car pulled up in the drive.

From Sophie's point of view, the news was the very worst—Ellen had found her ticket and money on the dressing-table, and sent Sam off with it to Hereford. Mortified though she was by the trouble the Bateses had taken for her—all for an entirely fictional crisis—it was nothing to the complexity of her feelings now she found herself left entirely to the mercies of Alex. Ellen's offer that she should phone Hereford station with a message for her husband to leave the money and ticket at the office there was met with a blunt refusal by her employer, before Sophie herself had time to get a word in.

'There's not much point,' he said curtly. 'Sam'll be on his way back here already. Even if I set out for Hereford right now, there's no guarantee we'd meet him on the way. We'll wait until he gets back, and meanwhile

I'll ring the station and find out if he's left her money there.'

He strode off in the direction of the study, and she followed in his wake, to watch uselessly while he dialled the station number. She resented his decisive, efficient manner. It didn't escape her that where she made up her mind quickly on impulse—which too often proved to be a mistake—his swift, logical brain had grasped all the relevant facts before he made his decision. She obviously had more to learn than *The Successful Businesswoman* could teach her. How ironic that it should be Alex who could fill in the gaps.

It was clear from the conversation that Sam had already called at the station, and was bringing back with him not only her money and ticket, but her suitcase as well.

'You won't be able to leave before he gets back.' Alex's tone was intended to leave no room for negotiation. She was conscious of the way he was looking at her, his eyes taking in her bedraggled ends of hair, and the way part of the front of her blouse had plastered itself to her body. 'Why not change out of those wet clothes and have a bath while you wait? Ellen will bring your suitcase up when Sam arrives.'

Her quick getaway completely ruined, she still didn't give in without a struggle. 'If we set off now we could intercept him——'

'No, Sophie.' That was very final, and there was no mistaking the steely glint in his eye. 'There are a number of routes he could take once he's turned off the main road. I'm not chasing him round the county when all we have to do is wait here half an hour or so, and he'll be back with your stuff.'

She stared at him helplessly, latent hostility in her eyes. Fate had conspired against her—at the rate things were going, she'd be lucky if she got away at all that night—

but she couldn't help wondering if fate was operating with Alex's connivance. Now he knew she could offer something he wanted, he seemed as keen for her to stay as he had been earlier to get rid of her.

CHAPTER FIVE

'HALF an hour or so', he'd said. And nearly two hours later she was still waiting!

There was no sign of Rupert either. Had he appeared, she was sure she could have persuaded him to set off in search of Sam. Hanging around doing nothing while she imagined herself missing yet another train was infuriating—she had resisted Alex's suggestion of the bath, in the hopes that Sam would reappear at any moment. Her clothes, now crumpled beyond redemption, had dried on her.

She began for the third time with increased emphasis, 'Sam must have broken down—we *have* to go and look for him!'

His eyebrows shot up at the imperative edge to her tone, but his reply was cool. 'I've told you before, Sophie, he'll find some way to ring. Wait.'

'But I have to be in London tonight! I could still get a taxi...' She glanced at her watch, then met his uncompromising stare with a stubborn look of her own.

'What's the point of that when Sam still has your stuff? And how are you going to pay for it?' He was forcing her to ask.

'You could lend me some money?' She eyed him defiantly.

'If you're short of cash, you'll just have to take the job I've offered you, won't you?' There was a certain satisfied finality about that. It had the effect of making her want to refuse the work forever and ever there and then—he was far too sure of getting things his own way!

'That's not the point,' she said crossly. 'I'll pay it back when I get to my father's!'

'I'm sure you will,' he agreed. 'But what's the hurry? Why get an expensive taxi all the way to Hereford when I'll give you a lift? Or Rupert will once he gets back.'

Slowly she was becoming convinced of the impossibility of her leaving at all, and she began to ask herself if she was merely sticking to the escape plan because it would prove more complicated to get out of it than to go along with it. But just sitting around like this she was playing into Alex's hands, allowing him to delay her until the urgency had dwindled into an anticlimax and she had decided she might as well take up the job he'd offered her. Clearly he'd classified her home situation as 'non-urgent'—if he believed in it at all. And while she had fidgeted around with nothing constructive to do, he had written a letter, and made a couple of phone calls. He didn't believe in allowing the unforeseen to interrupt the pattern of *his* life, and his efficient but relaxed attitude irritated her still further. It was time to make a stand.

She looked at him, reading a newspaper on one of the sofas. Any other man of his height half sprawled like that would have looked ungainly. Alex didn't. She tried to ignore the effect that powerful athletic body had on her nerve-ends, and stood up abruptly.

'My father's expecting me!' she began again.

'Ring him.' He flicked over a page of his newspaper. 'Tell him you'll be in London in the morning. You'll be no use to him arriving late tonight. Rupert will run you up to Hereford in time for an early train.'

His logic was irrefutable, but it put her on the spot: she couldn't admit that she wanted to avoid ringing her father from Derrham. The pitfalls, should the call be overheard, were obvious.

She clung to the thought that if Sam Bates returned soon there was still every possibility of catching a reasonable train. Once she reached Hereford station, she could warn her father of her plans in comparative privacy. The discussion circled once again, and she got nowhere.

'It's far more sensible to call from here,' Alex insisted finally. 'Use the phone in my study.' Something in his tone warned her not to prolong the argument any further, and he'd got up to hold the door open for her. Trying to oppose his will, she thought ruefully, was a bit like trying to swim your way up Niagara Falls. She gave up the unequal struggle, and—metaphorically speaking—resigned herself to drowning.

He didn't even leave her alone to speak to her father, but followed her into the study, and she got the feeling he was checking to make sure she put the call through, after such long and determined opposition.

It was the first time she had seen the room from which he conducted most of his business while at Derrham. Like the rest of the house, it was finely furnished, but the shelves were stacked with directories, and there was an impressive array of office equipment. It was orderly and businesslike, with enough that was individual to make it personal—a set of rare Japanese prints on the wall, Press cuttings in clips on the desk, and framed photographs. A picture of a little girl caught her eye. She had straight dark hair and a gap between her teeth—the elusive Louisa at last?

'Is this your daughter?' she asked, suddenly diverted by curiosity: this *was* an unexpected glimpse into Alex's private world!

He glanced at the photo in her hand. 'Yes.' His reply was short, and offered nothing more.

'And this?' She held out another—a snapshot of a very beautiful woman. She was dark-haired too, with dark eyes. 'Your ex-wife?' Somehow she couldn't believe it was Vicky—unless she'd dyed her hair. Where was the resemblance to herself which had caused Alex's extraordinary first reaction to her that day at the pub? She could never have been mistaken for this woman.

He glanced at the photograph. 'No.' Again he offered no further comment. A girlfriend, perhaps? He must have girlfriends—and of course they'd be sickeningly beautiful. She felt suddenly very uncharitable towards the dark-haired woman. Was there *any* one of life's little goodies that Alex Tarrant didn't have? There were other photographs, some of them featuring glittering social events. She picked one up. 'What's this about?'

'My company sponsored a big charity concert. That was a handshake from the grateful chairman.'

'And this? What were you being given an award for?'

His reply held a tinge of irony. 'Being able to make money.' And then he added pointedly, 'The phone books are beside the desk if you need them.'

'Thank you.' She hesitated, hoping he would leave, but he ignored her, leafing through the contents of a filing-cabinet drawer, apparently absorbed in a search.

It would be extremely difficult to hold the necessary conversation while he was in the room. She toyed with the idea of dialling a number at random, and faking a call to her father. But that might prove more problematic than actually speaking to her unsuspecting parent: Alex couldn't fail to realise that there was no one on the other end of the line. She delayed a little longer, resenting his presence.

'Is this a map of Derrham?' An old hand-coloured map hung on the wall, showing a detailed plan of the buildings and surrounding land. Her quick eye noted at once a long passage that apparently led nowhere. 'What's this? A secret tunnel?'

'It is. The Tarrant answer to a siege. They simply took to the woods.'

She indicated the ornate scroll in one corner. 'What does the Latin mean?'

'You've heard the old saying "He who fights and runs away..."?' Alex asked laconically. 'Well it's the Tarrant family motto.'

'I thought you were proud of your ancestors!' she accused.

'You don't admire pragmatism and resourcefulness?'

'They sound like a lot of cowardly opportunists to me,' she remarked in scathing tones. She would surely be leaving within a couple of hours; it didn't matter how she might antagonise him now.

'So what's *your* motto, Miss Sophie Carter?'

'Try anything once.'

He gave her an amused glance. 'Like page turning?'

She failed to meet his eye. 'I'm in the process of revising it.' And changed the subject. 'Does this tunnel still exist?'

'It does, in a very dangerous state of near collapse. I don't advise you to go looking for it.'

'I wasn't intending to,' she replied shortly. 'I'm leaving just as soon as Sam Bates can get back with my ticket, remember?'

He straightened up from the filing-cabinet, and gave her a long, thoughtful stare. 'I suggest you ring your father.'

Since he still showed no signs of going, she turned her back to him, her fingers crossed that her father would be out, and reluctantly dialled the number.

Her heart sank as she heard the familiar voice on the other end of the line. The one solution was to launch in, without giving him a chance to reply, and then ring off—she could only hope there wouldn't be a return call to enquire about her mental health. She began with breathless speed. 'Dad...? I might not be home quite as soon as I planned. I hope everything's all right——'

Her father's surprise was undisguised. 'Sophie? I wasn't expecting——'

Acutely conscious of Alex's presence behind her—she couldn't have been more aware of him if he had literally been breathing down her neck—she cut him off. 'I'll ring you again—I just wanted to check everything's OK.'

'It's fine. Why the panic? Wasn't it the end of——?' He was going to say 'the week' in reference to her expected return, but she interrupted him again.

'Right, Dad. Sorry this is so short—I have to go now. Bye. Love to Aunty Chris!'

She could sense his amazement—it must have been five years since his sister Christine had visited them—but she didn't give him a chance to comment, dropping the receiver like a hot potato.

She found Alex's gaze on her when she turned round.

'That was quick!'

'I—er—didn't want to waste the phone money.'

'Oh, I think we could afford to let you have that one on the house.'

She would have reacted to that as being unacceptably patronising, but for the unnerving impression that he had been able to interpret the whole conversation with accuracy, and was highly entertained.

It was another hour before there was a telephone call from Sam Bates, confirming Sophie's prediction that something had happened to the elderly Land Rover, and relieving them all of an unspoken anxiety on Sam's account. The vehicle had broken down in a lane on the way back from Hereford, and he had managed to push it a few feet off the narrow road towards the ditch, in which it was now neatly wedged. He had had difficulty in finding a phone, but finally had succeeded in contacting the breakdown services. Rescue was on its way, and it was only a matter of half an hour's wait or so before he would be back at Derrham.

Sophie was consumed with guilt. Her hasty reactions had put the Bates couple to an enormous amount of trouble, and now it had grown so late that there would

be little chance of catching a train even if she chose to
revise her plans yet again. She would just have to accept
the fact that she was staying the night at Derrham.

Following Alex's earlier suggestion, she decided to
have a long and leisurely bath—it was also a good way
of avoiding unwelcome conversational topics with her
host. She was still lying in the warm scented water,
reading a thriller, when Ellen tapped on the door to tell
her that Sam was back, and that all her missing be-
longings had been returned to her room. The housekeeper also offered to put the clothes she had worn that
day into the washing-machine.

'Only it's late now, and I can't stay to take them out
of the machine. You'd best get them out yourself, Miss
Sophie, if you don't want them too crumpled. I'll iron
them for you in the morning if you like.'

'Thanks, Ellen. Don't worry about the ironing. I'll do
it!' And with no sense of urgency now—it was far too
late to leave Derrham—she lay back again, for another
luxurious wallow.

It was ten o'clock before she remembered the clothes
in the scullery. Wrapping herself in a bath towel, she
tucked in one end to secure it, and made a cautious sortie.
The passage lights were on. The towel was only just
decent, and she was barefoot, but there had been neither
sight nor sound of Rupert and she was sure she could
dodge Alex if necessary.

She made her way down to the kitchen and into the
scullery. The clothes she had worn that day were still
damp, lying at the bottom of the washing-machine, and
she transferred them to the tumble-drier. She made
herself a cup of coffee while she waited, and sat down
sideways at the big table in the kitchen, pulling a lamp
towards her while she began to puzzle out the crossword
in the newspaper Ellen had left.

She was so engrossed that she didn't hear Alex come in, until a sudden lapse in concentration caused her to look up, and her heart gave a little jump of shock.

His raking gaze was taking in every detail, from the tumbled blonde hair straggling over her shoulders to the elegant length of bare legs stretched out in front of her. She could almost *feel* his eyes on her. He was standing in the doorway, some distance from her, but it was as though the space between them had instantly received an electrical charge. She couldn't believe he wasn't aware of it too. Then he met her eye, and his words sounded like a direct challenge.

'Who are you waiting to seduce?'

Afterwards, she didn't know what had got into her. Her only excuse was that one attack provoked another, and he had made her so self-conscious that it was difficult to think straight. 'You!' she said, in a tone she hoped dripped with sarcasm.

'Try anything once?'

She didn't like the sardonic blue gleam that accompanied that. He came into the kitchen, and, pulling out the chair opposite her, sat down at the table. 'Rupert back yet?'

Nervously, she watched him stretch out, his feet beneath the table and his arms behind his head, hands at his neck. She heard his muscles crack. She shrugged—carefully; the towel was precariously hitched. 'I don't know.'

She looked down at the crossword, pretending to concentrate on it. He hadn't as yet taken his eyes off her, and she found his gaze very disconcerting.

'All you need is a few puffing cherubs.'

'What?'

'That well-known Botticelli. "*Venus at the kitchen table*". Your hair's the right colour. Only she didn't bother with the purple towel.'

Could that *possibly* be an Alex-style compliment? Help! Supposing he took her seduction remark seriously? She tried to sound offhand. 'You're as bad as Rupert.'

'A good deal worse, I hope,' he replied smoothly. 'I've got a ten-year advantage.' There was a pause, then, 'Had any more thoughts about the restoration work?'

She hedged. 'What sort of thoughts?'

'Will you do it?' He was certainly persistent.

'I'll... have to have another look at it before I decide. It's a big piece of work.'

'It is,' he agreed. But he seemed satisfied by that answer and didn't renew the subject.

She was relieved she had got away without committing herself. She still needed more time to think. She felt very uncomfortable with him, too aware of her skimpy towel, and the fact that he was no more than a few feet away from her. Supposing he *was* taking her challenge seriously? She wished she'd never opened her mouth! There was a brief silence, then he said, 'Let's have a look at that.'

He indicated the crossword on the table, and she pushed it across, spreading it out and angling it towards him. He leaned closer to examine it, and then reached to turn it more comfortably in his direction. As he did so, his fingers lightly brushed hers, almost in the manner of a careless caress.

She started as if shot. For one crazy moment she wondered if he'd done it deliberately. The light touch had spread that intense awareness through her entire body. She regretted now that first provocative reply, and she gave him a startled glance. He looked up from the paper, a slight frown on his face, his eyes meeting hers, uncomfortably direct and very blue.

'What's the matter?'

'Nothing,' she said quickly, looking back at the paper.

He made no reply, and she didn't dare look at him openly, but when she ventured a glance in his direction

she could see one corner of his mouth curved the way
it did when he was amused. His attention was apparently on the crossword, but he seemed to have been able
to read her with uncomfortable accuracy.

'OK,' he said at last. 'Five down: Large store which
customers leave in frenzied state . . . Departmental.'

But as he took the pen from her he was careful this
time not to touch even her fingers as she passed it to
him, and it was that, if nothing else, that told her he'd
read her earlier reaction. Although it suggested that first
contact had been purely accidental, it didn't make her
feel any more at ease.

She watched him write in a clue, and then he turned
towards her, one elbow propped on the table, the other
on the back of his chair. His eyes fixed her, their expression as usual difficult to read.

'You know,' he said slowly, 'I don't believe a word of
this Rupert business.'

'Which business?' She tried to sound innocent. She
hadn't been prepared for the remark, but she had guessed
instantly what he meant.

'This engagement,' he said shortly.

Several things flitted through her mind at once: the
fact that the charade had for some time now been a considerable nuisance; the need to keep up the fiction at
least until Rupert came home, because she couldn't
handle the consequences if Alex had taken her provocation seriously; and a passing idea that maybe she owed
it to Rupert anyway to consult him on the subject before
finally admitting the deception. She played for time.
'Whyever should you think that?'

'You,' he said.

Her clear brown eyes met his in surprise. They assessed each other in silence, and it took all her nerve not
to look away. Again she felt that strange tingling feeling
beginning somewhere deep inside her. The lamp cast a
warm glow over the table, and tinged Alex's skin with

a deeper shade of bronze. His eyes were that unfathomable deep-sea-blue, and she couldn't read their expression. Her mouth felt dry.

Involuntarily she ran her tongue across her lips, and
then let her gaze fall—she didn't want him to take that
as a sexual provocation, nor did she want him to read
what she was now feeling.

Abruptly he pushed the paper towards her and got up.
'That's my contribution for tonight—you can solve the
rest yourself! Your clothes were ready five minutes ago,
by the way.'

But before he could make a move to go there was a
noise at the back door, and Rupert strode into the
kitchen. His astonishment at finding them there was obvious from his expression.

'Gosh, Sophe! A leg show! Trust me to miss the best
of the evening's entertainment!'

Alex gave him a shrewd look. 'Then you don't object
to your future wife entertaining another man in your
absence?'

For a moment Rupert looked nonplussed. 'What? Oh,
no—I'm not jealous-husband material.'

Alex looked as though he was trying not to smile, and
she was sure the exchange reinforced his conviction that
there was no engagement.

The pianist sat down, demanding a history of the day's
events, and Alex, though previously on the point of an
abrupt departure, favoured him with an account of her
abortive trip to Hereford station. It was something she
would have preferred to tell Rupert herself—preferably
with Alex out of the room.

'Come on, Sophe!' Rupert protested at once.
'Whatever possessed you to ring your father at all when
we were having such a good time here? You can't go.
You promised to turn pages for me and come to the party.
I'll tell you what it was—you had a row with Alex while

I was out and you're running away from him. You don't
have an aunt!'

She was sure he didn't believe what he was saying, but
she couldn't look at Alex—it was far too close to the
truth for comfort! Besides, he had overheard her curious
conversation with her father earlier, and in order to take
up the tapestry work as soon as possible—if that was
what she *was* going to do—she would have to invent
another phone call tomorrow.

'Of course I've got an aunt!' she asserted; it was the
one statement she could truthfully make. 'Just because
it upsets your page-turning plans! Why not ask Alex to
turn for you? He's obviously the expert. I can't even
read music, remember?'

She ventured a sideways glance at Alex to see how he
took it this time, but couldn't interpret his expression.

The state of play between herself and Alex had altered
so radically that there was no longer the necessity for
her to leave. Now the problem was how to stay without
being made to look a complete fool.

She was awake half the night wondering how she could
make a second and fully convincing phone call, to find
Aunty Chris miraculously recovered, and at the same
time hint to her father that she hadn't gone completely
mad. If only she could ring him without an eaves-
dropper! She could explain about the complications of
the evening before, and let him know that her stay was
being prolonged.

Finally she came to the conclusion that by far the
easiest thing to do was to *pretend* she'd rung him. She
was obliged to admit the truth to Rupert, and he nobly
perjured himself for her sake at breakfast, when the
question arose of her departure.

'Her father says the situation is no longer urgent,'
he explained to Alex blandly. 'A cousin——' an inven-
tion of his own '—is coming to look after
Aunt Caroline——'

'Christine!' she amended hastily.

'Christine. So Sophe can stay.'

'Sophie.'

The correction was Alex's this time. She had noticed before that he never shortened her name—it was one of the few things she would admit to herself she liked about him. She was uncomfortably certain that the deception hadn't taken him in for one minute. She was sure she had detected a fleeting grin on his face at Rupert's slip, and she tried to avoid his eye unsuccessfully.

'So this means you can start on the tapestry today, does it, Sophie?'

Their glances locked. Well, yes. That was what it did mean, but she'd forgotten that. Staying at Derrham of course would amount to her acceptance of the job.

The challenge in Alex's eyes was blatant. 'Another few weeks and it could fall off the wall,' he pointed out uncompromisingly. 'That's the general message I got from you yesterday.'

During that ill-fated conversation on the stairs, which had resulted in her putting everybody to a lot of trouble. Before she looked away, she was sure she could read exactly the same thought in his eyes that must have been all too apparent in hers.

'It's not quite as bad as that,' she admitted, 'but it is a long job, so I suppose the sooner the better.'

That finely sculpted mouth twitched, but he had the grace not to laugh. 'I'll get Sam and a couple of the men to take it down this morning. They'll have to bring the ladders from the stables.'

She was glad he didn't make his satisfaction too obvious.

But her sense of relief was short-lived. A phone call took him briefly from the kitchen, and in the interval she was grilled by Rupert on the subject of the previous day's events. Then Alex's sudden return interrupted her edited replies.

'What exactly did you say was wrong with your aunt, Sophie?' he asked, propping himself against the door-frame and folding his arms. She realised afterwards that the sheer casualness of the question should have put her on her guard.

'I didn't,' she said with no more than customary caution. 'It was—er—a touch of pneumonia.' The first ailment that came to mind.

'But she's all right now?'

'Oh, yes. It was a false alarm!' she assured him blithely.

'I thought you said she'd had a slight accident?'

She'd forgotten that! 'She fell over from weakness.'

His expression didn't change. 'I see. Your father seemed to think she'd be more likely to be suffering from a bout of alcoholic poisoning. She lives well, your aunt, apparently.'

'My father...!' She gazed at him in horror, the embarrassing truth only too clear.

He didn't even smile. 'Mmm. He was glad that he'd been around to offer succour when needed—and even more relieved to hear your aunt had recovered.'

'To offer succour when needed'... Just the sort of phrase her father *would* use!

She could actually feel herself turning scarlet. Alex's seriousness never faltered, but she had no doubt he was enjoying himself at her expense.

'I will say one thing for you, Sophie,' he commented coolly. 'There's never a dull moment when you're around.'

'I hate you, Alex Tarrant!' Just at that moment she wasn't sure she could identify what she felt exactly, but 'hate' would save further analysis.

'Bad luck, Alex!' Rupert commiserated with a broad grin. 'You haven't got a hope with Sophie—you're too far from her ideal man... What was it, Sophe?

"Comfortable old jerseys and reading glasses—the sort of man you can trust"?'

Alex gave his brother a keen look. 'I'm surprised she gave you so much as a second glance, then—let alone wanted to marry you.'

Rupert, edging towards the kitchen door, assumed a mysterious expression. 'Ah, but you make no allowances for my considerable charms...'

His exit was remarkably slick, and he made his escape via the kitchen garden.

This time she felt seriously annoyed with him: once again he'd left her with the lie to keep up, and then had repeated something she now regarded as a confidence— she didn't want such cherished ideas held up to the mockery of a man like Alex.

He lost no time. 'What's this about moth-eaten jerseys, Sophie?' he demanded. 'You can't be serious.'

She stared at her hands on the tablecloth. She'd had enough now of his amusement at her expense. His former hostility seemed to have changed into something new— this tendency to find her a source of entertainment, almost as though she were a precocious child he was hu- mouring. She'd resented his earlier attitude, but in many ways this was just as bad. Again it undermined her, and it didn't have to mean he had altered any of his previous attitudes towards her; he just wasn't taking her seriously enough to let them count.

He must have read her expression accurately. 'What's the matter?'

She examined the tablecloth minutely. 'I don't like people being rude to me,' she said slowly. 'Or about me. I know very well you don't think I'm good enough for Rupert, but you needn't make it so obvious!'

'I haven't said a word about Rupert!' he objected.

'You don't need to.' She could feel herself growing hot and flustered. 'You've already made your views per- fectly clear. And you don't have to make it so obvious you doubt my ability professionally either. People who have rarer and more valuable things than you have trusted me with them!' That wasn't strictly true, but she was beginning to warm to her theme. Without warning, all her resentments seemed to be boiling up at once.

He raised an eyebrow. 'But I thought we'd settled that. I've just given you the restoration work here, haven't I?'

'Yes,' she agreed reluctantly.

'So what's really eating you?'

There was a long pause. Scarcely twenty-four hours had elapsed since she'd walked out of Derrham, and once again they were at crisis point. What *was* it about Alex Tarrant that had such a disastrous effect on her? It was true, he hadn't said anything about Rupert. And he had given her the job—though if she wasn't careful she could talk herself out of it within seconds.

Why couldn't he read between the lines for once? Surely he must see that to be treated first of all as someone else, then to be classed as a joke, wasn't being considered a person in your own right? It meant that all the while he was coolly detached from her, discounting her from his scheme of things, except when she annoyed him, or amused him, or he could make use of her. But she, Sophie Carter, didn't really matter to him. That was what got her. Whereas she—well, what did she feel? One moment she found herself hating him, and the next . . .

She took a deep breath. She might as well admit it.

'I just get the feeling you don't take me seriously— on any level!' she said accusingly. 'As far as you're concerned, I might as well be some half-baked sixteen-year-old!'

A look of surprise crossed his face, then his eyes, very blue, raked over her. 'I wouldn't say that!'

'There you go again!' she said bitterly. 'Now I'm just a "bit of skirt" . . .' It was a phrase Rupert had once

used. 'An empty-headed...' What was it? 'An empty-
headed and self-seeking Vicky clone!'

She could see she'd got him there! He was visibly taken
aback, and she saw a muscle in his cheek tighten. He
knew now she'd overheard those unflattering remarks
he'd made not so long ago, and if he hadn't been Alex
Tarrant he'd have blushed for them. Moreover, the reference to Vicky was guaranteed to produce a reaction.

There was a loaded silence, and then, instead of the
attack she was anticipating, he said, 'You're mistaken,
Sophie.' His eyes held hers. 'I do take you seriously—
very seriously indeed!'

No apology, she noted. But she must have scored a
point somehow, because his answer was a lot more
careful than she'd expected.

'Well, perhaps you could show it by treating me as a
person for once—a person in my own right!' she added
meaningfully.

He didn't reply immediately. He seemed to be studying
her. Then he said, 'Exactly how would you like me to
put into practice this "person-treatment"?'

She wasn't sure what to say now; she was running out
of steam. She gave an exasperated sigh. 'Oh, I don't
know! I just...' Just what?

And then something dawned on her—something so
obvious that she couldn't understand why she hadn't seen
it from the first... If she didn't care about Alex Tarrant,
then it shouldn't matter to her one jot what he thought
of her. But it did matter—very much—because she
wanted his good opinion. And because, very far from
hating him, she was extremely attracted to him. So what
was really getting to her was the fact that he didn't seem
to be in the least attracted to her!

'Would you say you were treating *me* as a
person?' he enquired, when the silence had
lengthened considerably.

She tried to gather her wits. 'Not much different from the way I'd treat Rupert if he behaved as you do!' And I could kill Rupert just at the moment, she added mentally.

'Ah. Your fiancé,' he said. And that was all. She had no idea what that was supposed to mean.

CHAPTER SIX

Now that Sophie had recognised her strong and confused feelings about Alex for what they were, she found her new knowledge very inconvenient. Determined to betray nothing of the knife-edge awareness of him it gave her, she found it hard to act naturally in his company. And she didn't even *like* the man, for heaven's sake!

At his insistence, they went to the stables after breakfast with Sam and two other estate workers to look for the ladders. She would have got out of it if she could; Alex was far too good at reading her thoughts for comfort, and he was paying her more attention now— 'person-treatment'? She tried to adopt a polite aloofness, but it proved difficult to keep up.

The stable buildings lined three sides of a cobbled yard, but there were no signs of any horses—most of the loose boxes were being used to store tools and there was even a large motor mower in one of them. The tack-room smelled of bran and old leather and mice.

'Don't you keep horses any more?' she asked him, when her absence of reply to his commentary was becoming noticeable. 'I wish I could ride.'

He looked amused. 'I thought you were a city girl, Sophie! Long nails and high heels aren't standard equipment for someone with ambitions to muck out stables!'

He was getting at her again.

'I didn't say I wanted to *work* with horses!' she shot back defensively. 'I just meant I wanted to learn to ride them. And I'm not a city girl—I spent the first ten years of my life in the country.'

Unexpectedly, he smiled, his eyes, catching hers, a very deep blue again. 'How's *The Successful Businesswoman* coming along?'

'Fine,' she said, with renewed coldness. And then grudgingly admitted, 'I'm not sure I've got the right instincts for driving hard bargains.'

The quality of his smile altered. He was openly amused now. 'You seem to be doing all right to me! But you should advertise. Send round a brochure to the dealers— they often buy in stuff that needs repair. You'd only have to get a bit of work from a couple of them, and your name would get known.'

His tone was encouraging, but it was the advice of someone who didn't have to count every penny the way she did. 'I couldn't afford any glossy brochures,' she said with scorn.

'You wouldn't have to,' he replied coolly. 'You could set it all up on a suitable computer. Try it out in the study here if you want to.'

She was surprised by his offer, and was forced to the conclusion that he was taking her remarks at the breakfast-table seriously. But, afraid of betraying in any way the attraction that wasn't mutual, she showed no enthusiasm for his suggestion, examining instead the old bridles that still hung from their pegs. One with a coloured headband had a notice above it in large capitals: 'GOOFY'.

'Who's Goofy?' she asked. 'What a name for a horse!'

'My daughter's pony.'

'What happened to him? Has she still got him?'

The subject of his daughter had not been one he was willing to pursue the last time it had arisen. It was worth testing just how far his new communicativeness would extend.

He was looking at the bridle, a sudden harder light in his eye; she guessed she'd touched that raw nerve again, but as he turned to look at her she thought she could see pain in those blue depths. And he gave her more of an answer than she expected.

'When Vicky took her to the States they left the pony behind. Louisa should be spending half her time here, though Vicky chooses to ignore that, and it's something I've had to take up again in the courts—I don't want to upset Louisa with the ongoing rows all this has caused. So I'm hoping now it's just a question of time before she gets a chance to ride him. The Honourable Betty has him at the moment for her grandson.'

'Who?'

'Betty Laitham—the lady with the "dawgs".'

There was a ghost of a grin at that piece of mimicry, and he caught her eye. It was the sort of remark Rupert might have made, and she was aware for the first time of ways in which Alex might resemble his brother other than in looks.

She considered the Goofy story. It was an indication of the depths of his attachment to his daughter that he was prepared to fight again for her in the courts, and keep a pony she might be too big to ride by the time he got her back.

'How long is it since you've seen Louisa?'

'Almost a year.' There was something bleak in that, so she didn't pursue it.

'And the pony's name?'

He shrugged. 'My wife thought he had a stupid expression, and the name stuck.'

'My wife', she noticed. Not *ex-wife*. She experienced an unexpected little stab at that: Vicky, who had walked out on her husband and denied him his right to see his child, still figured in his conversation by a title to which she no longer had any claim. Could he, despite everything—all the bitterness and pain—*still* love her? It might account for the disinclination to marry again that Rupert had commented on.

Once the ladders had been transferred to the house, it took four men, with Rupert, Ellen and herself in attendance, to get the hanging off the wall and into the dining-room, the table having been moved to one side to allow it to lie on the floor. They all stood round it, staring first at the large expanse of dusty needlework, and then at her.

Alex, hands on hips, looked at her quizzically. 'So what happens now? You're the boss.'

She eyed him with hostility. The unexpected reversal of roles—'person-treatment'?—wasn't going to convince anybody. While he remained there he was a challenge to any authority she might assume. She wished he'd just leave her to it.

However, it was under her instructions that they rolled the tapestry carefully between layers of old sheets, parcelling the outside to protect the backing, and after a brief telephone call she arranged for the hanging to be collected two days later. Barring unforeseen problems, it could be delivered back within a fortnight. It was the first time in the chequered history of her relations with Alex that she'd been able to show that she could do anything with efficiency—even if he did undermine her self-confidence.

He was studying her with that acute attention she found unnerving.

'What next?'

'Well, nothing really until it's cleaned. I could go home for a while.'

Those dark blue eyes seemed to challenge hers. 'Or I could give you some more work to do while you're waiting—interested?'

What was this—finding things for her to do to keep her at Derrham? But she shouldn't flatter herself; Alex was merely making the most of his own business opportunities.

'I might be,' she said carefully.

'Your *Successful Businesswoman* would tell you seize every opening.'

'I do.'

'I wouldn't classify a half-hearted "might be" as a sign of insatiable business-hunger!'

She bit her lip, determined this time not to let him get to her with that critical tone.

'She'd also tell you to plan your work so that you don't waste time,' he went on. 'And there's a piece of needlework in one of the rooms upstairs I'd like you to look at—you might be able to mend it. You can add the repair work to the final bill.'

Trying not to be irritated by the way that everything he said sounded like an order, she followed him upstairs. He had long legs, and on the steps above her his height seemed to dominate her.

She hadn't been into many of the other rooms, and this one looked as though it had been recently refurbished, though the bed in it was the genuine article. With its carved posts and massive wooden headboard, it was certainly impressive.

'Looks wonderful, doesn't it?' he commented. 'But I'd defy anyone to get a good night's sleep on it.'

She glanced at him, and then at the bed, and it was at that moment that something very disconcerting happened. As she looked at the wide four-poster, she was embarrassed to find herself imagining what it would be like to be lying on it with the tall, dark and powerfully attractive man standing next to her... Shocked by the vivid sensuous quality of her own thoughts—and that it should be Alex who provoked them—she glanced up guiltily, to find him looking at her oddly. There was something in the nature of his silence which made her wonder whether he hadn't been able to read the images straight out of her mind.

Telling herself firmly she should have far more control over such inconvenient reactions to him, she approached the foot of the bed, and with an effort turned her attention to the superb hangings. Automatically her professional eye noted how badly the colours of the old embroidered curtains had faded, and how one in particular was in need of skilful repair. But underneath she was still intensely aware of the man behind her.

She glanced round the room and commented as casually as she could, 'All this looks as though it's been very recently redecorated. It's beautiful. Who designed it?'

He followed her, to stand behind her again, and instantly she was conscious of just how close he was. 'What's happened to your ambition to change it all once you're Mrs Rupert Stretton?' he demanded.

'Er—that was before I saw Derrham...' Her voice sounded very uneven, betraying her sudden nervousness. Strange little prickles were running up and down under her skin, and her heart seemed to be beating more quickly. 'I could never manage anything like this... Was the designer your wife?'

'My mother,' he said shortly. 'Vicky's ideas and mine didn't coincide.'

There was a pause while they both appeared to be considering the bed hanging again.

'Can you do something with it?' he asked after a few moments. 'It's not so old—Victorian—but it's worth preserving if possible. It was once a very fine piece of work.'

That was her idea too, but she hadn't imagined he would have been so perceptive of the beauties of the embroidery. She was surprised—but that was typical of Alex. Just when she was struggling to come to terms with one set of reactions to him, he'd show another side of his nature that undermined all her efforts. She took a deep breath, trying to ignore the insistent pulsing in her veins. 'So your mother's redecoration is post-Vicky, then?'

He nodded.

'I'd quite like to meet your mother.' Her reply was as much for something to say as to voice any genuine interest. She was feeling even more acutely those magnetic prickles all over her body, while a kind of weakness began to melt her from the inside.

His next words threw her completely. 'I think she might like to meet you.' It was the first time that he had shown any interest in including her in the family life of Derrham.

He was standing just behind her, so close that they were almost touching. One tanned, lean-fingered hand rested against a carved post of the bed beside her, and she found herself staring at the Tarrant ring that gleamed a dull rich gold against the dark wood. When she finally turned—intending to move away from him, to put a safe distance between them while her body was sending such wild signals to her brain—somehow she found herself with her back pressed against the post, Alex's hand by the side of her head.

She gazed startled into his eyes, tensely aware of every inch of him. For an age they seemed to be hanging on a cliff-edge of expectation.

Then he made a small movement towards her that brought his body up against hers, and before she was aware of exactly how it had happened he had trapped her, the carved wood digging into her back as his other hand clasped the post behind her waist, his arms forming a loose prison round her. The contact was electric.

He stared down at her, his eyes dark with thoughts she couldn't guess at, and, mesmerised by the look in those navy blue eyes framed by their long black lashes, she was too overwhelmed by the unfamiliar intensity of the physical contact to make any move. Her heart was beating violently as though it were going to leap out between her breasts—she was sure he could feel it pounding against him. Then he was looking at her mouth.

It flashed across her mind that she might be giving him such blatant signals that he was doing no more than react to them. But Alex wasn't a man to go along with anything passively, and the look in his eyes told her so. He was fully aware of what he was doing, provoking her, playing his own game, and it was too late by the time it dawned on her that by just letting him tantalise her like that she was telling him what he wanted to know.

She knew what he intended to do, but even while something in her was hating him for it his mouth touched hers, and her whole body seemed to catch fire. For endless seconds she seemed to be fighting the sheer physical insistance of it—and then unwillingly let him part her lips, giving herself up to the sensations that were sweeping through her.

He made no move to take her in his arms, to caress her, even to touch her further, but there was nothing tentative or exploratory about his kiss, leisurely though it was; it was as expert and thorough as if she had been his lover. She had had no idea that a mere kiss could be like that—an invasion of mind and body that admitted no denial, that demanded every bit as much as it gave. Then he drew back.

It took a moment for her to register the completeness of that withdrawal, his sudden and total non-involvement. She stared at him in shocked silence, her blood still racing in her veins and her limbs turned to jelly. Only one kiss and she had almost been ready to give herself to him—and he surely knew it!

He said nothing, watching her through narrowed eyes. It was only then that she began to realize how little he appeared to have been affected by what he had been doing—there was not a sign, unless it was the slightly quickened pace of his breathing. When he spoke at last he sounded completely calm, in control of himself and the situation, as he had been all along. 'Why did you let me do that?'

It was hard to utter a word. 'What?' she asked stupidly.

'I thought you were engaged to Rupert.'

Oh. So that was what it had been about. What a fool she had been—a complete and utter fool! Deliberately he had exploited that powerful latent attraction to satisfy his own curiosity. But while he had revealed nothing of himself except perhaps his calculation, any reaction from her other than cool indifference would only confirm what she had discovered from her own humiliating surrender, and what he must now know too: just how devastatingly attracted she was to him.

Rather than have him thinking she was a cheat, she could of course tell him the truth about Rupert. But she rejected that idea—it would be letting him get the better of her through his own unscrupulous methods, when all the time it was *he* who was the cheat, not she!

Of course, if she could bring herself to sink to his level she could do a bit of seducing on her own account. It wouldn't be too hard to end up with a genuine engagement to Rupert, and then the high and mighty Mr Alex Tarrant wouldn't act so smug! For Rupert's sake, she wouldn't do it, but there must be some way to score a few points at his expense.

Anger now fuelled her determination to make him wait for as long as she and Rupert could spin out the fictitious engagement, before she let him know she wanted nothing to do with the Strettons—or the Tarrants.

'I *am* engaged to Rupert,' she said, with an assumed and icy dignity that would have been completely convincing but for the tremor in her voice. 'Now you tell me something—what right have you to kiss your brother's fiancée like that behind his back?'

His eyes, holding hers, narrowed. 'I want the truth. And I haven't got it yet, have I?'

She stared him out. 'Ask Rupert!' she flung at him defiantly, and moved abruptly sideways to evade that casual and calculated embrace.

He caught her arm, his fingers squeezing her flesh painfully, and his eyes were cold. 'Don't play the outraged innocent with me, Sophie! It's a role that doesn't suit you after that last little exhibition! Let me point out the obvious for you—you *enjoyed* it.' The careful emphasis spoke volumes. 'Now I suggest you consider your future very seriously. Should you be thinking of marriage *to anyone*—let alone to my brother—when you're so willing to share your favours with whoever happens to come along?'

The insult stunned her—he was, in effect, calling her a whore! Did he really think so badly of her? Outrage mingled with humiliation choked her reply, and she turned on her heel and headed for the door. But underneath the turmoil of her emotions, hurt pride had determined one thing for her: if he thought she was going to run home this time, he was very much mistaken! Since there wasn't a lot worse he could say or do, she didn't have much more to lose!

For the next few days Alex remained at Derrham, his German trip hanging fire. She expected repercussions from their bedroom encounter—would she be shown the door, have the restoration contract terminated, or at very least would Rupert be forbidden to marry her on pain of exile?—but Alex made no reference to what had happened, nor did he show any signs of cancelling their business agreement. When he wasn't out on the estate, and she couldn't avoid him, she was guarded in her responses to him. She analysed his manner towards her for signs of the inevitable contempt, but at worst he merely seemed preoccupied, and most of the time she was forced to admit that he treated her very much as previously. Perhaps he had always regarded her as a potential whore, so the revelation of her supposed duplicity towards Rupert had come as no surprise.

Then guests arrived for lunch, at his invitation. The couple, Helen and Paul, lived locally and they brought with them another friend of Alex's. Gaby.

A little older than Sophie, her spectacular blondeness reducing Sophie's warm honey-coloured hair to mouse, Gaby looked every inch the photographic model she was.

Sophie, present as the guests arrived, was obliged to watch as Alex greeted Helen first, and then Gaby. His voice had that deep, smooth tone that was one hundred per cent seductive. 'Ah—Gaby, the green-eyed siren!' Sophie couldn't miss the light of appraisal—and approval—in his eyes. 'How's the international cover-girl this week?'

Gaby laughed, and returned his kiss of greeting with interest. She was nearly as tall as he, and Sophie, hating him, was unexpectedly and inconveniently agonised with jealousy to the point of indigestion. She had to admit to herself that they made a marvellous couple, though. Gaby was as strikingly blonde as Alex was dark.

'This is Sophie,' Alex was saying. 'She's doing a bit of expert stitchery on our mouldering heirlooms.' Alert for an Alex-sarcasm at her expense, she noticed Gaby give her one keen glance as they shook hands. But it was the assessment of a potential rival—then Gaby dismissed her. Obviously she couldn't compete with such fashion-plate looks, and didn't therefore feature as a serious threat in the model's mind.

That annoyed her. Prompted by something she didn't stop to analyse, she announced sweetly, 'I'm Rupert's fiancée!' And then looked directly at Alex.

His face gave little away, but she thought she could read surprise—and some hostility—in his eyes. There were predictable exclamations from the others, and congratulations which she accepted with a certain relish, but she was sure Alex was thoroughly disapproving behind the urbane mask.

She made her escape as soon as the introductions were over, and could hear Gaby laughing at something Alex had said as she ran up the stairs to carry on with her work. No doubt he would be suave, entertaining, amusing—all the things he never bothered to be with her. Well, good luck to Gaby! she thought vindictively. She would soon find out what a callous, calculating customer he was behind all that wit and charm!

Gaby and her friends left late that afternoon, and she continued to avoid Alex, using her work on the curtain as an excuse. She kept a careful record of the hours, determined to present a businesslike invoice at the end of it. There was no further mention of her brochure, and she didn't think he would bring up the subject again. His offer had been before the scene in the bedroom, and before she had so defiantly publicised her 'engagement' to Rupert.

Alex had passed no comment on that, to her surprise, but just to be on the safe side she had warned Rupert of what she had done. As she expected, he found it a good joke, and it was with difficulty that she dissuaded him from following it up with a fake announcement in the newspapers.

When she wasn't working on the curtain she was with Rupert, practising page turning for the recital. She was needed only for one piece, but once again it was only with practice that she could judge where to turn. But although outwardly she appeared busy, inwardly she was continually preoccupied. Alex had taken over her mind. During his absences she found herself resentfully wondering what he was doing, and his image—tanned, lean and good-looking—was perpetually in her thoughts.

In the past she had had what she now dismissed as 'adolescent' romances, although the first had been when she was eighteen, and the second nearly three years later.

She realised now how incomplete each had been, and, in comparison with Alex, both the men she had fallen for had been boys.

Inexperienced, despite her confident manner, and uncertain of herself, she had kept her first real boyfriend at arm's length. In her relationship with her second, too, she had been undecided, unable to commit herself to someone she didn't really trust; good-looking men like Tony were far too sure of their own attractions, and it was after he had broken off their relationship that she had developed the image of her ideal man—cardigan, spectacles and all—someone not so very different from her father, totally and predictably *safe*!

But Alex wasn't safe—far from it! He was the most devastating man she was ever likely to meet, and their closer encounters had proved pretty disastrous. Had it been merely a matter of intense sexual attraction, somehow it wouldn't have been so bad. But there was more to it than that. If she'd had any sense of self-preservation she'd have left Derrham for good by now, despite Rupert and the restoration work, but Alex had a power over her she couldn't define and she couldn't resist. He scared her, and excited her, and infuriated her, and most of the time she found herself hating him. But skirmishing with him had that exhilaration of fast skating, with Alex himself all the darkness under the ice—and just as dangerous. And every now and then her brushes with him explored something in herself she hadn't known was there. But it made her feel very insecure.

'Is that the dress that merits lettuce-leaf lunches—the one you thought you might fall out of?'

Halfway down the staircase on the night of the concert, with Rupert behind her, she found herself suddenly caught in Alex's critical blue gaze, as he stood in the hall taking a detailed inventory of her appearance.

For her, at least, relations had reached such a strained pitch between them that she felt she couldn't afford to give an inch, no matter what it cost her. She was determined he wouldn't make her blush for her past remark, or for the fact that her glamorous display of bare shoulder was far from the self-effacing garb of a dedicated page turner. After all, she was a legitimate guest at Betty's dance, wasn't she—whatever Alex might choose to think of her? She stared back defiantly. 'It is!'

'I don't think there's much danger of that. It isn't so bad after all.'

She wouldn't admit even to herself that she was secretly hoping he might pay her a straightforward compliment. Trust him to put a sting in the tail!

'Thanks a million!' she said grimly. 'You do a lot for a woman's confidence.'

'You don't need compliments, Sophie. You know you look good. It's written all over you!'

His voice was light and teasing, and he seemed to be in an unusually good mood, but she refused to be amused. He could see through her far too easily, and it wasn't fair of him to show her up in a way that made her look vain and silly. Especially when, more than ever tonight, he seemed to radiate the kind of power that spelled experience and success, undermining her own rather shaky confidence. The severe black of his dinner-jacket emphasised the darkness of his hair, and the white evening shirt flattered further the deep golden tan of his skin.

She had thought that Rupert in his 'concert rig' as he called it—'Just to give Betty a thrill'—looked fairly spectacular when he came upstairs to fetch her, but beside his brother he was scarcely even remarkable.

She was just about to give Alex a stinging reply, when the doorbell sounded. As they all glanced instinctively towards the entrance, Alex taking a stride towards the door, a woman appeared in the inner doorway. She hadn't even paused to be admitted.

Sophie recognised her at once. She was the dark-haired woman in the photograph in Alex's study.

Despite the incident of the blonde, green-eyed Gaby, it had never occurred to her that he might invite someone to partner him to Betty Laitham's dance. Right up to the last moment he had given no hint of it, and, although she'd supposed she would be naturally paired with Rupert in his mind, in her own mind the unattached Alex still presented her with that secret, dangerous challenge.

But if Gaby could be seen as a threat, then there was no word that adequately summed up her first feelings about this woman...

Her photograph had scarcely done her justice. She would have been beautiful at any age, and in any century. She was in her thirties, her black dress sophisticated and expensively cut, but, with her waist-length dark hair, and dark eyes, she looked like a girl.

'Bronwen!'

Rupert leapt down the last three stairs as one, to fling his arms round the slim figure extravagantly, but, despite the theatricality of his welcome, it was Alex's greeting that particularly struck Sophie. The kiss he gave the beautiful brunette was neither passionate nor even intimate, but it spoke a very deep affection, and she could read clearly genuine emotion still in his eyes as he turned back to where she was standing at the bottom of the stairs.

'Bronwen—this is Sophie.'

The fleeting expression of surprise on the other woman's face quickly turned to a look of frank curiosity.

'Sophie's here to mend the tapestry,' Alex was saying, 'among other things.'

There was no time to analyse that last comment. Bronwen was smiling and holding out her hand.

'At long last! I've been telling him about that tapestry on the stairs for months—I thought it was going to fall down before he did anything about it!' Her dark eyes caught Alex's, and he laughed.

'I got the same message from Sophie—but her suggestions were rather more practical than yours!' His remark alluded to a shared past in which she could have no part, and there seemed to be a private level of communication between the two of them that excluded even Rupert.

Sophie felt a little knife twist somewhere inside her. This was a feeling very different from the straightforward jealousy she had felt towards the predatory Gaby. Very different... With her photograph in the study and familiar access to the house, it was obvious that Bronwen had a very special place in the life of the owner of Derrham.

CHAPTER SEVEN

'AH, THE waif at the railway station!' Betty greeted her bluntly. 'Get back to Derrham all right?' Standing in the flower-banked hall of Betty's rambling and impressive Queen Anne house, Sophie couldn't help noting the way Betty's eyes, as she made the remark, went to Alex. He was standing just behind her with Bronwen; Betty's look of curiosity was the same look Bronwen had had. It was getting to be irritating, this feeling that there was some kind of mystery everyone else knew about, and she didn't.

Repressing an impulse to ask about the health of the 'dawgs', she supposed she said all the right things, because seconds later every thought was wiped from her head but one. Betty was greeting Bronwen, and not only was it obvious from the quality of her welcome that Bronwen was a member, like the Tarrants and the Strettons, of the county social world in which Sophie herself had no part, but also that there was more—a great deal more—to Alex's relationship with Bronwen than she had guessed.

'And has he finally got round to it?' Betty was demanding. 'When are we going to be able to dust off our wedding hats?'

Bronwen smiled, looking happy. 'I'm not saying!'

'She deserves the best!' Rupert said.

It was then that Alex put his arm round her waist protectively, pulling her against him. 'She certainly does,' he agreed. 'Here's to the second time around!' And Bronwen laughed, leaning her head on his shoulder.

The second time around... It could only mean one thing! The unexpected stab of that curious knife inside her once more told her that for all her anger with Alex, simmering away underneath the aloofness to him she had now adopted as her habitual pose, she was fooling herself if she believed for one moment that his insulting behaviour to her in the bedroom had rendered her indifferent to him. It must be jealousy she was feeling—an intense jealousy that actually hurt so much that at first she could hardly bear to watch him with Bronwen.

It hadn't occurred to her that the relationship might have gone that far; Rupert had told her from the first that his brother had showed no signs of finding another wife. But had he known about it all the time? A glance at the pianist didn't reveal a man in a state of shock—if he hadn't known of it, it was certainly no surprise to him. He might have warned her! She felt very resentful towards him all of a sudden.

But there was a curious twist to the whole thing. Unlike the polished and sophisticated Gaby, Bronwen was sweet and quiet in her manner, and drew openly affectionate treatment from both brothers, not just Alex. There was no hostility in her attitude towards Sophie herself, and it was impossible not to warm to her; Sophie's generous nature instinctively wished her well, despite her more painful feelings.

But towards Alex she couldn't bring herself to feel half so charitable. She thought of the way he had flirted with Gaby—was that fair to the woman he was going to marry? And much, much worse: there was his behaviour towards herself! Whatever his ulterior motive at the time, it had been unforgivable to kiss her like that when he was all but engaged to Bronwen. His behaviour towards both of them was callous in the extreme.

Page turning for Rupert after that was a very different experience from the recording session. Alex, standing at the back of the room, caught her eye as she made her

way up to the little platform, and she interpreted that
blue glint as a sardonic one. No doubt he was thinking
of her last 'performance' in the recording studio. She
did her best to appear unaffected by it, but in reality she
was fiercely preoccupied almost the whole way through
the recital with thoughts of him and Bronwen. They were
sitting together in the third row. She could turn almost
automatically now, but never once, even when she had
nothing to do, did she let her gaze stray to the audience.

Alex's and Bronwen's engagement must still be un-
official—there was no general talk of it. Rather like her
own 'engagement' to Rupert, she thought ironically;
gossip about that couldn't have got around yet. And it
was then that the idea occurred to her...

While Rupert bowed and smiled, she mulled it over,
and, although her body followed him into supper at his
insistence, her thoughts, angry and confused, were with
Alex. She watched him covertly whenever she could, as
the plan began to form in her mind.

The buffet supper was followed by dancing. The
former ballroom had been emptied of all its drawing-
room furniture. It glittered with chandeliers and mirrors,
and glass doors opened on to the terrace, where lanterns
had been hung along the side of the house. A string
quartet was seated in an alcove at one end of a room,
and as soon as they struck up a familiar Scottish reel
tune Rupert grabbed her.

'Come on, Sophe! This one's for us!'

She didn't want to dance—not with Rupert, anyway—
but she was glad of something to occupy her until she
had a chance to put her plan for Alex into operation.
She looked round several times for him, and eventually
caught sight of him at the far end of the room. He was
with Bronwen, and they seemed to be in the middle of
an absorbing conversation. He had his hand on her
shoulder, and suddenly she looked up at him
and laughed.

She kept a bright, and secretly empty, smile on her face as she contemplated her plan of revenge. She would sit out the next dance.

The tunes changed, to old-fashioned polkas and Viennese waltzes, and Rupert, losing interest, wandered off to find some more champagne, promising to bring her a glass. She sat down in the little sitting-room that opened off the ballroom, and, finding herself alone, kicked off her shoes, throwing herself back in a comfortable chair and swinging her legs over one arm of it. It was a relief to be alone, even for a few seconds. She was still thinking about her plan. It was a pity Bronwen was so nice. She deserved a better character than Alex for a husband! Never mind, her revenge wasn't going to hurt Bronwen; it might even benefit her in the end, although she wouldn't know about it. It was only meant for Alex. Tit for tat, she thought with a certain satisfaction.

She caught sight of herself in a large gilt-framed mirror. She felt hot, but she looked unusually pale. She sat back again, fanning herself with a magazine she had picked up from a small table, and waited for Rupert to return with the champagne.

When a man's figure appeared in the doorway, she looked up quickly, and her heart gave a little leap. It was Alex, not Rupert. She felt her sense of purpose weaken. He was too handsome, too dynamic, too treacherously attractive to her for her to retain that inner indifference that was vital to her revenge. And there was something about him tonight that she could only attribute to his happiness at being with Bronwen. But she told herself that what she was going to do was for Bronwen's sake as much as for her own.

'Rupert abandoned you?' Alex lifted one dark eyebrow quizzically. 'What about a drink?'

'I'm fine, thanks.' She pretended to glance at the magazine, praying Rupert wouldn't come back too quickly. She had to appear suitably indifferent, so it looked like entirely his idea.

'You don't waltz, Sophie?'

'Rupert doesn't. Anyway, it's time to take a rest.'

'But what about you?'

She glanced at the dancers through the doorway, with what she hoped was a wistful expression. 'I learned to do an ordinary waltz, but I've never done all that whirling around!'

'Want to try?'

It was what she had been waiting for! She didn't want to admit to herself that lurking somewhere underneath her revenge was a suicidal desire to feel Alex's arms around her just once more, no matter what the consequences. Anyway, to refuse would be unnecessarily ungracious, and she wasn't *obliged* to put her plan into operation if she didn't feel like it...

She gave an elegant shrug of her slim shoulders. 'Yes, why not?'

She got up, and fished under the chair for her shoes, conscious of him watching her while she slipped them on.

'Let's dance here,' she suggested. The small sitting-room would give them temporary privacy, and she didn't want to draw anyone's attention. She needed time alone with Alex if her ploy was to work. 'I might bump into people if we're out in the middle.'

'You're supposed to follow, not lead!' he pointed out crisply. 'You like being the one in charge, don't you?'

'So do you!'

He looked amused, and nodded towards the whirling couples. 'Seen any candidates tonight for the baggy-cardigan-and-spectacles romance?'

'Of course not!' That image would never be the same again—he'd completely destroyed it!

'I suspect you're looking for a wimp so that you can keep the upper hand.'

She protested at once. 'I'm not looking for a wimp! I'm not "looking for" anybody!'

'I forgot. The search ended at Rupert!' His eyes narrowed speculatively. 'You should have played the field a bit more, Sophie. I don't expect an embroideress, or whatever you call yourself, gets to meet many people. You must have spent most of your time stitching.'

Not *again*! She was really fed up now with his attempts to break up a relationship that didn't even exist, but at least it gave her a relatively safe area in which to skirmish. She couldn't retaliate on the Bronwen front—yet.

'I've got a lot of friends . . .'

'People like Rupert?'

She looked him dead in the eye. 'Do you mean to imply that I could do better than your brother?' *Now* tell me to my face I'm not good enough for your family, Mr Alex Tarrant!

His reply wasn't along the lines she'd expected. He was taking her seriously. 'Rupert's too young for you. He's still got a lot of growing up to do.'

Taken aback, she stared at him—his eyes were that dark unfathomable blue again.

'I seem to remember you commenting once before on my youthfulness, so what's the magic difference between twenty-one and twenty-four, when the twenty-four-year-old happens to be me?' She had a very clear idea about that difference with regard to herself and Rupert, but it would be interesting to hear Alex's version. She got the uncomfortable feeling now that he was looking right into her.

'You may not be as grown-up as you like to think, but I don't imagine that whatever process is left is going to change you very much. It's not the same with Rupert. Speaking from experience, I'd say that twenty-one was far too young for the average man to think of marriage.'

Speaking from his own experience with Vicky? That bore out what Ellen had told her.

'Here's to the second time around' he had said.

'I'm very happy as I am, thank you,' she replied shortly. Or at least I was until I met you. 'I don't want to make any changes.'

He looked amused again, the more serious mood suddenly vanishing with the sideways twitch of his mouth.

'So what about this dance, Miss Carter?' She felt the pressure of his hand under her elbow, and, without waiting for her reply, he began to steer her towards the door. 'We can't waltz in here—there's no room.'

'What about the terrace, then?' she suggested quickly. 'I don't want people gawping!'

He glanced at her in mild surprise. 'Don't want to be seen with L-plates on? I thought you had more nerve than that, Sophie!'

She restrained her immediate impulse to hit back at that one, and he guided her round the edge of the ballroom in the direction of the glass doors. Her plan looked as though it might work!

Outside the summer evening was heavy with the scent of roses. Leading the way, she headed for the far end of the terrace, out of sight of the ballroom. A flight of steps led down from the raised terrace, towards a lawn and a little summer-house. They could still hear the music clearly. It was an ideal spot, provided no one decided to follow them. This had to be a very *private* revenge!

'Here?' she said. She was very nervous. They were several feet apart, but she felt he was too close.

He held out a hand to her. 'Lesson one—you have to come a lot nearer than that!'

With reluctance, she moved a bare inch in his direction. Faced suddenly with the reality of six feet one of male dynamite at such close quarters, she knew she would never be able to resist the sheer physical magnetism he possessed for her. Her hand met his. In a manner she hoped was cool, but feared he would interpret correctly as tentative, she put her other hand on his shoulder. He had taken a step towards her, and they were almost touching. If he had been the devil himself, she could hardly have been more nervous of coming into contact with him.

'Don't be such a little virgin!' he teased softly. His voice had that low, mellow tone that was like honey in her veins, but she found his words rather shocking—they were more suited to a man intent on seduction. What about Bronwen—surely he hadn't forgotten her already? Well, he deserved what was coming to him!

'You can't waltz if you're going to keep a "proper" distance,' he pointed out. 'I bet you wouldn't be so stiff with someone you'd met in a disco!'

'I wouldn't expect someone I'd just met in a disco to want to dance so intimately close!' she retaliated.

Alex's sideways smile told her he was, as usual, deriving considerable amusement at her expense. 'I wasn't asking you to dance "intimately close", but dance with me in an acceptably formal manner. And what's this about "just met?" I'd say we were old sparring partners by now, wouldn't you?'

She didn't know how to answer that. 'Sparring' with him was not what she had in mind—to begin with, anyway.

As he drew her against him, she wondered if he would be able to sense the dizzy rate of her pulse. She was acutely conscious of one tanned, lean hand resting low on her bare back. 'Ready?'

Initially, she tried to resist the contact, but held so closely against him from the waist down, she could feel every contour of muscle and every movement of his thighs as he whirled her round. It was both impersonal and astonishingly intimate, and, despite her cold-blooded plan, from the very first few steps all her determination to keep him at a safe psychological distance began to ebb away.

She had had no idea that an old-fashioned waltz could be so sensuous. The way he seemed to be able to control all her responses to him, he could have been making love to her. He was subtly guiding her across the terrace, and all she had to do was let him lead her. She didn't even have to know the steps. All too quickly the stiffness melted out of her and she let herself get caught up by the intoxication of the movement. The tide of music seemed to rise higher and higher in a flood of romance and excitement, and she had a struggle to remind herself that it was just a dance, and that somehow she *had* to get her revenge for the way he had insulted her. And she would also be striking a blow for Bronwen.

But if it hadn't been for her plan, she would have made up her mind there and then that her first dance with Alex would be her last. It was the kind of exquisite torture all through that she didn't want to have to repeat, but there was scarcely a break as the next waltz started up, and this time she found herself being drawn into it inexorably.

'You can't pass a test on just one lesson!' Alex said, almost in her ear. She wasn't sure if it was her imagination, but he seemed to be holding her even closer this time. In theory it was just what she wanted, but in practice it made her wary. Surely he wouldn't be succumbing to the seduction of it all so easily?

'This is supposed to be the most dangerous dance in the world,' he told her, looking down at her, a quizzical expression on his face as he whirled her round. 'Did you know it was banned when it was first introduced? Want a rest?'

She nodded, speechless, and followed him down the steps towards the summer-house.

Then she realised she'd made a mistake. The two garden chairs set out invitingly for a tête-à-tête beside the lawn were no good for her purpose—she needed to be in Alex's arms for what she intended to do, not sitting next to him having an informal chat. Also, the small lawn with its surrounding flower borders and high box hedges, although suitably romantic and enclosed, was too visible from the terrace.

The flowers, very white in the gloom, were roses, and she sniffed at them at random, wondering how to lure him further away from the house without her motive appearing too obvious. Then, almost on cue, he provided the excuse for her.

'Has Betty shown you her garden before?'

'This is my first visit. Are you offering a guided tour?'

'I thought you wanted a rest,' he pointed out.

'Only from dancing.'

He appeared to consider her for a moment, and then led the way towards a flight of steps to a lower level.

'I'm surprised Rupert hasn't brought you here,' he commented. 'Betty's spent years building up the garden on this hillside. There are wonderful views in the daytime.'

Now there was only a soft darkness that stretched towards Wales, hiding the valley, and a hint of stars as a backdrop. Ideal! But how was she going to inject that undercurrent of seduction into a conversation that was so unpromisingly neutral? They'd be discussing the weather next. She wished she had more experience; Alex was no fool, and his unexpectedly obliging mood only made her the more uneasy with him.

They reached a grass path between herbaceous borders, and, glancing back up towards the upper lawn and terrace, she judged they were well out of sight of the house, though the music from the ballroom was still audible. It provided her with the opportunity she needed, but she had to steel herself. Her heart seemed to beat faster rather suddenly.

'Let's dance here!' she suggested. 'Along this path!' She turned towards him, and put a hand carelessly on his shoulder, as though it had just occurred to her.

Alex laughed, and she couldn't tell whether the idea genuinely appealed to him, or whether he could see right through her. 'What was wrong with the terrace?' he demanded. 'This is very uneven.'

'It doesn't matter—it's more fun here!' She began to hum the waltz tune that was floating down from the distant ballroom, and, nerving herself for what she hoped was to follow, she took a step that brought her up against him.

Her thighs against his, her whole body seemed to come alive with a dizzying intensity that reached right through to her bones. She was never going to be able to keep up a pretence of detachment when his mere touch could do this to her!

The corner of his mouth quirked as he looked down at her, and she felt his hand at the back of her waist. 'Ready?'

She gave him a smile she hoped he would find seductive, and, pressing herself against him as closely as she dared, let him lead her in the first steps of the dance. The lawn was uneven, as he had said, but from her point of view that was an advantage, and when she missed her step she had a perfect excuse to cling to him more tightly. In response, his arm tightened round her in support, and he stopped.

There was a pause, while he seemed to be considering her. She let her eyes slide sideways, looking up at him under her lashes. It felt like an age, and she wondered if she should make a move first—but it had to look as though the idea had come from him.

'Why do I get the feeling it isn't dancing you're after?' he asked softly.

'I don't know!' she said, in a voice that was almost a whisper. 'Why do you?'

He was still holding her very close, and his eyes glittered in the darkness as he looked down at her. Then he laughed. 'Sophie—you're irresistible!' And as though in answer to her unspoken wish, he drew her closer, and bent his head, his mouth instantly finding hers.

She could hardly believe her good luck—it was exactly what she had planned! But in that first moment she was too startled by the immediacy of it to respond. Then she was afraid that he might back off, and let herself return his kiss, relaxing against him—she had somehow to get him to give her a *real* kiss, one that would compromise him fully!

His arms tightened again, and as his lips began to move gently on hers she could feel his fingers slide down her bare back, caressing her spine. She felt a little surge of triumph at his response, but she wasn't sure how far to encourage him—she was already far too deeply affected by him, her body clamouring for more. That melting weakness was flooding through her, despite her determination to keep aloof. He knew exactly how to evoke the desire that was already latent in her—and when he was only amusing himself with her it wasn't fair, it just wasn't fair!

She could feel the heat of his body even through his clothing. She tangled her fingers in the thick, silky hair at the nape of his neck, urging him to a further response, and he began to kiss the side of her jaw, and then the line of her throat. His lips felt cool against her skin, and she had no idea whether he was genuinely caught up in what he was doing, or cynically testing how far she would let him go, but she didn't dare prolong the experiment. It took every ounce of will-power she possessed to hold to her plan. With a sudden and rather desperate resolution, she pushed herself away from him, and twisted out of his grasp.

She stopped just out of his reach, breathing quickly. She couldn't read the look on his face in the half-darkness, but her own eyes glittered in excitement and triumph.

'*Now*, Mr Alex Tarrant,' she announced breathlessly, 'we're quits! You accused me of playing fast and loose with Rupert, but what about you? You're engaged to Bronwen!'

She couldn't of course have expected a shock-horror reaction from someone like Alex, but, faced with the threat of immediate exposure as a two-timing philanderer, he might have registered some convincing expression of dismay.

'I see!' he said, with disappointing mildness. 'The "people in glass houses" ploy? That's blackmail, Sophie!'

'Yes, isn't it?' she agreed. 'But I got the idea from you!'

He thrust his hands casually into the pockets of elegantly tailored black trousers, his shirt-front suddenly very white in the near darkness. He seemed to be breathing rather quickly too, but perhaps that was her imagination.

He assessed her. 'So what's the price of your silence?'

'Your future good behaviour, of course!' she said tartly. 'If you try to behave like that with me—or anyone else—again, I'll make sure Bronwen knows about it. She deserves better than that!'

'And supposing I told you that Bronwen wouldn't mind my kissing another woman?'

'I wouldn't believe you!' She managed to sound quite contemptuous. 'I'm sure you'll find that Bronwen underneath is just the same as everybody else. She'll want you to yourself!'

'Are we talking jealousy here, Sophie?'

'We certainly are! And if I were you I'd bear that in mind!'

'I will—I *am*,' he said smoothly. 'It's been most enlightening!'

It wasn't the conclusion to the interview she'd planned. Although she hadn't exactly envisaged reducing Alex to a guilty heap, she had expected to unnerve him, at the very least. But he was disappointingly unmoved. The only reaction she could detect in him was one of amusement. She hoped it was just a mask for his secret discomfiture, but she wasn't convinced. Her only recourse now was a hasty retreat while she could still claim to have scored a point or two.

She gave a shiver that wasn't entirely pretence, and said in tones that did credit to the acting ability Rupert had admired, even if the excuse was a bit lame, 'It's chilly out here now—shall we go in? I told Rupert I'd dance with him again.' And, avoiding his eyes, she turned back the way they had come.

It was only when she met a blank wall that she realised she had missed the steps back up to the upper garden. She hadn't been paying much attention to the layout on the way down.

Alex was standing waiting for her some distance back along the grass path. He made no attempt to disguise the amusement in his voice this time.

'It's this way, Sophie!'

She approached him slowly, trying to appear unconcerned, and intending to sweep past him up the steps and back towards the terrace. But as she drew level with him, keeping the maximum distance between them that the narrow grass path would allow, his hand shot out to grip her upper arm. She gave a gasp, and then found herself being drawn towards him. It wasn't a development she had prepared for.

'Now,' he said, 'let's find out a little bit more about this jealousy, Sophie. Could it be yours, I wonder?'

She couldn't resist the force with which he turned her to face him—she'd never have believed the strength in those lean, tanned fingers.

'Ouch! Let go, Alex ...!'

He looked down at her. 'Then you stop fighting me,' he suggested, his voice like silk.

He held her hostile gaze for what seemed like an age. Initially she didn't know how to react. She wasn't sure what he was going to do.

'I wasn't fighting!' she began. 'I was——' And she found the rest of her protest smothered before she could utter it. His mouth covered hers, his fingers still grasping her arm.

She did her best to remain uncooperative, holding her body rigid and trying to turn her head away, but it was a futile resistance, almost childish. She felt his fingers, hard on the side of her jaw, and then the grasp on her arm slackened before his other hand slid up into her hair, so that she was doubly locked into his embrace.

But that first punishing kiss was quickly over—he was far too experienced not to be able to get the better of her without force. He began a second assault on her senses, more gently this time, by subtle persuasion gradually winning a response from her, so that when he finally released her she could scarcely stand. It was just like that time he had kissed her before, in the bedroom.

Afraid her knees might buckle under her if she tried to walk away from him, she remained, staring up at him, her lips slightly parted. This hadn't been part of her plan at all! she thought dazedly. It was he who should have been compromised by a display of passion, not she!

He had made a pretty clear statement that, whatever her feeble attempt at blackmail, it could have no effect on him. If there was any threat, it worked the other way: it was she who was the vulnerable one. And by demonstrating just how easily he could affect her physically, he had also made out a pretty good case for sexual jealousy. So who was teaching whom the lesson?

'Had enough of the games yet, Sophie?' he enquired softly.

She didn't know what he meant by that, and she didn't wait now to find out. His words suddenly brought home to her just how he had succeeded yet again in humiliating her, and she broke out of his grasp, turning quickly and unsteadily towards the steps. She was sure she heard him laugh as she reached the top of them. It was all she could do not to run.

In bed that night hurt fury—with herself and with Alex—kept her awake. Once again nothing had worked as she had hoped. With his curious reaction to being caught out in such obvious deceit, instead of admitting guilt, he had succeeded in turning the situation to his own advantage.

But it didn't quite add up somehow. If he was engaged to Bronwen, and she had no doubt he was, why hadn't she scored the points she had expected? And why had he allowed himself to be led into a compromising situation with her at all? The more she considered it, the more of a complete bastard she thought him. For him, there was clearly no such thing as commitment to one woman. Poor Vicky—no wonder she had divorced him! And poor Bronwen—he was already having fun behind her back. But Sophie Carter he had already written down as a whore, so whatever might be her feelings in the matter wouldn't count anyway!

Her relief that he was not at breakfast the following morning was short-lived. She met him on her way to the library, where she had left her work. He was coming in through the front door, and looked in very good spirits. That made her even more resentful. She attacked before he could. 'Back from a night on the tiles?'

'In a manner of speaking. I stayed at Bronwen's.' She was uncomfortably aware of his scrutiny. One dark lock of hair had fallen on to his forehead; it made him even more attractive to her, despite her immediate feelings. She knew he had driven Bronwen home from the dance,

but not that he was intending to spend the night at her
house. She felt both angry and depressed: it seemed to
confirm irrevocably their relationship, and that the precarious hold she had hoped to gain over him had failed.
He was virtually flaunting the fact.

'How did you enjoy the dance?' he asked, watching
her too closely for her liking.

'Wonderful, thank you.' She avoided meeting his eye.

He laughed. 'Get out of bed the wrong side? Or is it
all that champagne I saw you drinking at the end of the
evening?'

She ignored that. She wasn't going to admit to a
hangover. Assuming a detachment she was far from
feeling, she launched into a carefully prepared question
that left him no opportunity to introduce any topic other
than her restoration work. She had a strong suspicion
that, given the smallest opening, he would say something she would rather not hear.

She did her best to avoid him after that; it helped considerably that he was out to dinner the two following
nights, and during their brief subsequent meetings such
remarks as they exchanged began to resume the barbed
quality of her earlier days at Derrham. From her point
of view the situation could best be described as 'armed
neutrality', and the cool, amicable manner he had
adopted towards her since the dance became gradually
more aggressive as she kept up her defences.

It was three days later that he came to find her in the
library as she was working. He shut the door behind
him, and leaned against it, hands thrust into his trouser
pockets. The air was instantly charged with little hostilities, and she wondered if he had come to declare open
war. But his first words were a complete surprise.

'What do you think of being mistress of Derrham
for a while?'

She stared at him, her brown eyes full of mistrust. Could this mean at last that he was going away on that long-delayed German trip?

'Rupert has a series of concerts in London for the next couple of weeks,' he went on, ignoring her lack of response. 'I'll be away for five or six days. Do you mind being left alone in the house? You can spend the night with the Bateses if you'd prefer, or Ellen says she'll come and sleep here. Unless of course you want to take the bed curtains up to your father's?'

Bed curtains. Had he introduced the topic deliberately, or was it a purely inadvertent allusion to the first time he had kissed her?

She considered his last suggestion, but the prospect of enjoying Derrham alone appealed to her. It would be a relief not to have to be continually on her guard.

'I'll stay.'

'So I can leave all my worldly goods in your capable hands, then?'

'I won't steal the pictures, if that's what you mean!'

'It never crossed my mind that you would. Keep the cannon on the roof loaded, repel all boarders, and remember the motto.'

'Yes. Cowards to the rear,' she said tartly.

For the first time since their exchange the morning after Betty's party, his eyes flashed an intense blue in the way they did when he was genuinely amused by something. 'I was thinking of *your* motto—but by all means try on the Tarrant maxims for size! Help yourself to anything you want, and consult Sam in any difficulties. Anything else I can tell you?'

'Your phone number?' she suggested coolly.

'I'm very flattered.' The smooth tones irritated her again. 'But will you have time for little chats if you're working?'

'I was thinking of emergencies. Dial a bedtime story— that sort of thing.'

He actually laughed at that, and wrote down a series of numbers with times and dates on a scrap of paper.

'Just ringing round those should keep you busy. I'll be leaving in about half an hour. Be good. What shall I bring back for you? Chocolates?'

She pulled a face. 'Gin would be more appropriate.'

It was a mutter for her own benefit rather than his—she absolutely refused to be won over by him—but it amused him again. He was standing over her now, watching her stitching. Then, without any warning, she felt the side of his finger flick her cheek.

The unforeseen gesture, which from anyone else would have been one of affection, suddenly froze her.

'Be good,' he said again. And he was gone.

She put up her hand to the side of her face, where he had touched her. What on earth had he meant by it? How dared he play with her feelings like that? The gesture was so uncharacteristic, so unexpected, that she spent a great deal of time angrily arguing with herself about the significance of it, and then gave up. She felt even less able than before to guess at his motivation. The only thing to do was to continue to pretend absolute indifference to him. That way he had no power over her.

Once both he and Rupert had gone, after a brief bout of loneliness she quickly adjusted to the peaceful silences of the old house, and immersed herself in her work, grimly determined to banish Alex from her mind. She saw both Ellen and Sam in the course of the day, and spent one evening with them at the cottage. Two days passed uneventfully. Then on the third afternoon something outside everybody's calculations occurred.

The sound of wheels on the gravel prompted her to get up from her seat and look out of the library window. Rupert back earlier than expected—or Alex? But a red taxi was in the drive, and, as she watched, a young woman got out, and then a girl, about eight or nine years old. The woman was quite pretty—another of Alex's admirers? She wore a loose-fitting jacket and jeans and there was something about her style that didn't look English. The girl too had long dark hair. She was very slim, and wore jeans and a lavender-coloured sweatshirt, and when she turned so that Sophie could see her face there was something instantly familiar about her. She looked discontented, and scuffed at the stones in the drive, while the woman appeared to be arguing with her.

Then the doorbell rang, and there was a long pause. The library was too far away from the hall for conversation to be audible. Then Ellen came to the library door.

'Sorry to disturb you, Miss Sophie, but I'm not quite sure what to do. Was Mr Tarrant expecting his daughter?'

Sophie stared at her blankly. *Louisa*? Could this be some devious plan of Alex's?

'He hasn't said anything to me,' Ellen went on doubtfully. 'The au pair that's with her says she's on her way to France, and she's been told to leave Louisa here. Her mother's on holiday. I was wondering if you knew anything about it.'

It looked now as though his daughter's arrival would be as much of a surprise to Alex as to Ellen and herself, otherwise he would certainly have told the housekeeper of it. Any mention of his daughter had seemed to evoke deep feeling in him—he obviously loved her dearly, and would surely have arranged to stay had he known there was a chance she might come to Derrham. The obvious conclusion was that Vicky must be making use of Alex; something had happened in her life, and eight-year-old Louisa was now an inconvenience to her.

On reflection, Sophie was slightly ashamed of her conclusions—how could she judge a woman who was a complete stranger?—but it fitted the image that had been built up of Alex's ex-wife.

She followed Ellen out into the hall. She was instantly aware of a pair of blue eyes like Alex's staring at her resentfully. Louisa Mary Tarrant looked like one very tired and uncooperative eight-year-old. Her face was pale and there were shadows under eyes, and she was scowling. Sophie couldn't help feeling sorry for her.

The French au pair didn't look very happy either. Sophie held out a hand. 'Hello—can I help? I'm a friend of Mr Tarrant's and I'm staying here at the moment. Hello, Louisa!' Her smile received no answer. The uncompromising stare never wavered while Alex's daughter considered her with a mixture of suspicion and resentment.

'Mrs Tarrant ask me to bring 'er 'ere,' the French girl began at once. 'She 'as to go away and can't take Louisa. I too cannot stay wiz 'er. I ave to go 'ome to France. Mrs Tarrant say that Mr Tarrant will be 'ere!'

No amount of explanation could persuade the au pair to change her plans, and stay the night. She merely looked at Sophie in despair.

'But I 'ave to get my train!' she protested. She looked genuinely distressed, and Sophie felt sorry for her too. It wasn't her fault.

She glanced at Louisa, who was examining the hall now, under her eyelashes.

'Can you wait while I try to contact Mr Tarrant?'

The French girl looked at her watch hurriedly. 'Only a few minutes please!'

She rang the most likely number Alex had given her, but succeeded in speaking only to his secretary. Alex was in a meeting—no, she didn't know when it would finish. Could she take a message?

Sophie debated the wisdom of announcing through one of his office staff the arrival of his daughter, and decided against it.

'Just tell him Sophie Carter rang, could you? Perhaps he could call me back when he has a moment!'

CHAPTER EIGHT

IT WAS a couple of hours before Alex contacted her, and meanwhile she and Ellen were left to deal with Louisa. The au pair was gone again within minutes of her arrival, after giving the totally unresponsive Louisa a peck on the cheek. '*Au revoir, chérie*. Be good.'

It was impossible to tell whether the child had any feelings at all about the matter. She remembered Ellen, who made a great fuss of her, but failed to give more than a token response to her. Towards Sophie she was positively hostile.

'What are you doing here?' was her first accusing greeting, and her unnerving stare was oddly reminiscent of the curious looks she'd had from just about everyone who knew Alex, and met her for the first time. Who on earth was it she was supposed to look like? Some controversial ex-girlfriend of Alex's?

If Louisa was looking for a confrontation, she took the wind out of her sails completely with her reply. 'I just work here,' she said mildly. 'If you get bored any time, perhaps you might like to help me mend a few things.'

Louisa gave her a withering look at that.

Fine, thought Sophie, if that's the way she wants to play it. Let Alex deal with her when he gets home!

She wasn't quite sure what would happen once Alex did get back. Louisa would have to stay, of course, but with the German trip in the offing he would have to take her with him, or make some alternative arrangements.

Louisa's first enquiry concerned the whereabouts of Goofy, but Ellen's assurances that he was being well looked after by Mrs Laitham didn't meet with a favourable reception.

'But he's *mine*,' Louisa insisted. 'I want him here! She's got no right to have him.'

'He was getting fat and lazy,' Ellen explained. 'I expect your father thought he could do with a bit of exercise.'

Louisa looked even less happy with that. Then she asked, 'Where is my father?'

'He's gone to London,' Sophie offered, drawing the fire from Ellen.

Louisa shrugged. 'Off with one of his women, I suppose.'

Yes, he probably is, Sophie agreed silently, and then met Ellen's shocked gaze over the girl's head.

'What makes you think that?' she asked carefully, hiding her own cynical response.

'Mummy said he was always off with women.' She sounded casually disapproving, with all the world-weariness of an experienced adult.

Louisa's attitude reflected Vicky's, but Sophie wondered instantly if the information was true. If Alex had been unfaithful, that might account for Vicky's bitterness over the marriage—removing the photographs from the family album—and the subsequent divorce. And if she wanted any proof about his cavalier attitude to the women in his life, she only had to consider his treatment of herself and Bronwen!

But after Louisa had gone upstairs to explore her bedroom, Ellen brought up the subject of her employer's alleged infidelities unbidden.

'It's not true that—about other women!' she protested, with fierce loyalty. 'I don't remember he so much as looked at anyone else all the time he was married to Mrs Tarrant! The boot was on the other foot if you ask me.'

'You mean Vicky was unfaithful to him?'

The housekeeper made a sound like 'Tch'; she wasn't going to commit herself that far, but her reaction seemed to confirm it.

As always, the sound of Alex's deep, attractive voice sent shivers down her spine when his return call finally came through.

'Well, Sophie, what can I do for you? Ringing to wish me the time of day, or is there a crisis already?'

'It's funny you should say that...' She tailed off, hostilities temporarily forgotten. She was wondering how best to convey the news.

'Come on, out with it. Ellen run off with the postman, has she?'

'No—no of course not. It's—well...' There was no other way to put it really. 'Louisa's here!'

A tense silence. Then he said, 'Alone?'

'Yes—no. Not exactly. She arrived with an au pair. Apparently her mother's had to go away somewhere, and she thought it might be a good time for Louisa to pay you a visit...'

He cut across her attempts at tact, that sarcastic note she hated back again. 'Thank you, Sophie. I appreciate your desire to paper over the cracks, but I'm quite capable of working out the situation for myself.'

'Don't take it out on me, Alex!' she flashed back at him. It had been a trying couple of hours. 'I'm only here to do textile-restoration work!'

There was another brief silence. Then his voice, rather tight this time, said, 'From that do I deduce the au pair has gone?'

'She seemed to have pressing reasons for getting back to France. She was here all of five minutes.'

'But Louisa's OK?'

'Not one hundred per cent happy with the situation, but physically, yes.'

There was another brief silence, and in those intervening seconds she had the impression that he was thinking out his strategy.

She was right. His tone was far more conciliatory when he began again. 'Listen, Sophie, I have to ask you to do me a big favour—you'll be doing more for me than you can imagine... The German business has come up at last.'

Somehow she could guess what was going to come next!

Without waiting for her reply he went on, 'That would mean the earliest I could get to Derrham would be Friday. Just look after Louisa until I get back from Munich, will you? I'd be coming down to see her, only I have to fly out there tonight.'

She was torn: although she felt sorry for Louisa, while the child was so hostile to her there would be little she could do with her or for her, and at a more complex level one part of her wanted to be won over by this new, less dictatorial Alex and gain his approval, while another part of her told her firmly she was being used.

It was as though he could read her line of protest in advance.

'I'm not asking you to be solely responsible for her—just be around, that's all. Besides, it's not fair to leave it all to Ellen—she's got enough to do——'

'And I haven't, I suppose?' she said tartly.

'Leave the needlework—you won't be getting the tapestry back for a while yet anyway, and the curtain can wait. I'll pay you as much for your time as you'd get stitching all day—more!' He sounded, for Alex, surprisingly urgent, and that got to her too. But money wasn't what she wanted—she didn't know what she wanted, except that it wasn't that. 'Louisa will like you. Take her out. If you need money, Ellen and Sam know where the keys to the safe are.'

'You could employ another au pair...'

'I don't want an au pair. I want someone I can trust.'
Was that a genuine compliment—or flattery?

'Why don't you ask Bronwen?' She tried to make that
sound as neutral as possible.

He sounded surprised. 'Bronwen? She'll be in
Germany.' She should have guessed that too.

'Sophie, I can't discuss this right now. I'm due in
another meeting in a couple of minutes——'

'I see,' she said in clipped tones. 'Business comes first.
And your daughter?'

She could hear him take a quick impatient breath. 'I'll
ring you back again later...'

She was about to say, Don't bother, when there was
a click and the line went dead. But whether he rang her
again or not, she knew just what the outcome would
be—she'd be looking after a sullen and difficult eight-
year-old for four days, and at the end of it would be
blamed for anything that had gone wrong.

'I'll pay you'... She didn't want him to pay her—the
very suggestion of it was insulting. By offering her money
now he was making it clear that he still had no personal
interest in her, while continuing to exploit the attraction
she felt towards him, of which he was only too well
aware.

And he had guessed, rightly, that once landed with
the task she wouldn't turn her back on it. She felt slightly
outraged—as usual, he had the devil's own nerve!

Louisa spent the rest of the afternoon in the kitchen
with Ellen, making pastry men out of spare dough. She
rejected all Sophie's attempts at friendliness, so that in
the end she gave up. She could understand the little girl's
feelings; she had been dumped by her mother on a father
about whom she must have heard little that was
favourable. She was a stranger in her own home, and
must feel rejected by both her parents.

Keeping an eye on Alex's daughter that afternoon
proved to be the full-time job she had feared, and again

it was difficult to find anything that pleased her. But an unexpected development was the appearance of Louisa at her bedside late that night. Sophie had been reading and was about to switch out her light.

'What's the matter?' she'd asked with concern. 'Don't you feel well?'

Louisa said nothing. She looked thoroughly forlorn, and there were traces of dried tears on her cheeks. Sophie guessed she felt lonely and frightened, and missed her mother. Her heart went out to her, and a strong—though hitherto unexplored—maternal streak prompted her to pull back her duvet.

'Come on, love,' she said. 'Hop in—this is such a huge bed that there's lots of room for two.'

Louisa hung back for a second, and then her thin little body was wriggling in beside Sophie.

She said nothing in explanation, but it seemed to establish a silent bond between them which became more evident once Alex was home.

His return was totally unexpected. Instead of staying away the four days he had planned, he flew home the very next afternoon. Sophie discovered subsequently that he had forced the first stages of the deal through with record speed, and left the finalising details in the hands of one of his directors. It said something, at least, for his concern about the situation at Derrham. She wondered why he hadn't brought Bronwen back with him—she had been in Germany, after all—but he made no mention of her.

His arrival had an interesting effect on Louisa. Her half-hostile, half-tolerant daytime attitude towards Sophie changed almost immediately, and she became almost inseparable from her. Her aggression was now spasmodically reserved for her father.

Sophie noticed the change from the moment Alex's familiar low white car drew up in the drive. Taking Louisa with her, she went to the front door to meet him.

She felt a stab of sympathy for Alex when, as he swept Louisa up in his arms, she presented one cold little cheek to his kiss, and afterwards ostentatiously wiped the side of her face with her sleeve. He looked exhausted. She saw his expression tighten, and a muscle twitched in his cheek. It was only too painfully obvious that Vicky had succeeded in driving an effective wedge between father and daughter.

'What's the matter, Lulu?' he said at once. 'Afraid I might turn into a frog if you give me a kiss?'

'Of course not,' she said, full of childish scorn.

'So you think you'll catch toad-warts or something, do you?'

He got a grudging smile for that, and an unwilling enquiry about the precise nature of the ailment.

Alex, it now emerged, had a vivid imagination which he explored to the full for his daughter's benefit. Sophie could see that, despite herself, the child was softening to his charm, and found even her own antagonism weakening under the force of it.

But relations between father and daughter for that very reason were uneasy. Allowing herself to be won round, Louisa felt disloyal to her mother, and would attempt to redress the balance by distancing herself again. Sophie had to hand it to Alex, though; his patience seemed endless—or almost.

There had been an emotional scene over Goofy, with passionate accusations from Louisa.

'But *why* did you send him away?'

No amount of explanation would satisfy her. It was impossible to decide whether she was deliberately stirring up the subject to harass Alex, or whether the whole matter had in reality caused her a deep and secret grief that was not yet assuaged.

But the biggest bone of contention proved to be the existence of the secret passage Alex had once mentioned to Sophie herself. Louisa had discovered its existence from Sam, and from day one of his arrival gave her father no peace on the subject. It was the one topic on which she was prepared to hold any sort of a sustained dialogue.

His tolerance visibly began to run out one night at supper. Hitherto Sophie had had to admire his forbearance when she herself might long ago have lost her temper.

'There is no secret passage.' His tone was curt. He wanted to get the subject over and done with.

'Bates says there is!' announced Louisa defiantly. 'He said it went all the way to Derrham village, and people used it to escape during the war.'

'The Civil War,' her father corrected.

'So there is one!' Louisa crowed triumphantly. 'I'm going to look for it. I bet Bates knows where it is!'

To Alex, and Rupert, Sam Bates was 'Sam', as much a friend as an employee. Louisa's habitual use of his surname could only have come from Vicky's influence. Now Alex's face darkened. 'There's to be no more talk of secret passages, and no searching around for them! Some of the parts of this house are very old, and any tunnel would have been blocked years ago. The building is no longer completely safe. I forbid you to go anywhere without Sophie—is that clear?'

'Then Sophie will help me look!'

'No, she won't,' Alex said shortly, with a warning frown. 'She knows better than to go rooting around in dangerous places for secret tunnels that don't exist.'

'What sort of dangerous places?' Sophie asked quickly. She could see from Louisa's face that there was going to be a real outburst any moment.

'Don't put ideas into people's heads,' Alex warned again. 'There's to be no unauthorised exploring—is that clear?'

'But if you told us where it was,' she suggested, 'there would be no need to go looking for it—and if it's

blocked, as you say, there'll be no point going down it.'
Tacitly, she was supporting Louisa's argument that the
passage existed, but to remove the mystery and challenge from the idea might deprive Louisa of much of
her incentive.

Alex's eyes, a dark, stormy blue, flashed his opposition to the suggestion, but he was silent for a moment.

'Right,' he said at last, 'if I tell you where it is, that's
an end to the matter. And I don't want to hear that anyone's been anywhere near it—OK?' Louisa nodded, but
Sophie was almost certain she had her fingers crossed
behind her back.

The revelation that the entrance was in the cellars was
made without drama, and the subject publicly dropped,
to Sophie's relief. But she felt obscurely responsible for
Louisa knowing about that tunnel now, a feeling that
was privately reinforced by Alex once Louisa had gone
to bed.

'I'll thank you not to undermine my authority again
in front of my daughter!' he remarked curtly. 'It's difficult enough to strike the right balance with her without
you encouraging her to defy me.'

'I wasn't doing anything of the sort!' she flashed back,
the truce they had achieved since Louisa's arrival now
broken. 'I just thought that making a big secret of it
would be bound to whet her curiosity——'

'So, since she now knows where it is, I'll hold you
personally responsible if she decides to go and explore
it.' The line of his mouth was hard, and his eyes a vivid,
angry blue.

She felt her colour rising. So much for short-lived
gratitude—you wouldn't think it from the way he spoke
to her, but she was doing this man a *favour*, for heaven's
sake! But she bit back the retort that was on the tip of
her tongue—there was no point making the situation any
worse—and left the room without a word.

If she hadn't been growing fond of Louisa, and felt so sympathetic towards her, she'd have walked right out of the house there and then, and *nothing* would have persuaded her to come back!

The problem of entertaining Louisa was an ongoing one. Despite Alex's renewed patience, there were occasions when his daughter resisted him completely. Sometimes he would be able to win her round without her realising she had fallen under his spell, but such lapses were inevitably followed by the periods of rebellion when she would shadow Sophie all day. Sorry for her, Sophie herself felt obliged to spend a great deal of time trying to amuse her rather than getting on with her work.

To her surprise, Alex encouraged her, and she wondered if he was now trying to make up for his ungrateful remarks. 'Leave the restoration for a while,' he told her. 'It's much more important you get on well with Louisa. I want her to feel secure here, but she still doesn't trust me...'

That makes two of us! Sophie reflected wryly, but she didn't voice the thought.

'I can't blame her—it's her mother's fault,' he went on in hard tones. 'She took Louisa in the first place partly out of spite, and she's had almost a year to set her against me.'

Vicky, it had emerged, had a new man in her life. He was rich and successful, with a grown-up family of his own, and had little interest in Vicky's eight-year-old daughter. They were on holiday together in the Caribbean, and conveniently Vicky had remembered that Louisa had a father on whom she could be dumped. Sophie couldn't help feeling sorry for both father and daughter. It was obvious that Alex adored Louisa, and his affection would have been fully returned had it not been for the complex question of loyalties. It was difficult to see how the situation could be resolved.

*   *   *

The treasure-hunt was entirely Louisa's idea. Alex had started the morning relatively high in her favour, but as the day progressed and he had been forced to refuse several of her requests through re-scheduling business since his premature return from Germany, her personal skies had darkened considerably.

'I could hide something, and you and Sophie could look for it,' she suggested. '*Please*, Daddy!'

Sophie guessed it was a last-ditch attempt for his attention, and she could see that he was torn. It was the first time Louisa had openly pleaded for anything.

'You'll have to start without me, sweetheart,' he said ruefully. 'I've got some musicians coming in half an hour—we're thinking of signing them up to make a recording.'

Briefly, her eyes lit up. 'A rock group?'

Alex grinned, and caught Sophie's eye over her head. 'I didn't think you were old enough to be interested in rock groups! But sorry—no. A couple of classical guitarists. They'll be here at three.' He glanced at his watch. 'If Sophie hasn't found the treasure by the time they've gone, I'll help her look for it.'

It was the best he could offer, but she could see that his daughter regarded it as a personal rejection. A sulky cloud settled over her.

She chose her "treasure" from a small console table in the hall: it was a heavy embossed solid silver vase, a regimental presentation to her Tarrant grandfather. She lugged it off the table and clasped it defiantly to her chest. It was obvious she was looking for an objection from Alex, but he took the wind out of her sails completely, merely pulling a wry face on seeing it and catching Sophie's eye again over her head.

'As long as you don't forget where you've hidden it!' he teased. 'And Ellen will do you in if you put the tiniest scratch on it!'

Louisa gave a small grin despite herself, but pretended to ignore him. 'Wait for me in the library!' she instructed Sophie. 'I'll come back and tell you when I've finished.'

'Just keep her occupied for a while,' Alex said when she'd gone. 'I'll give her some time as soon as I've got rid of these people.'

'Are you really going to sign them up?' she asked, curious.

'That depends,' he said shortly. 'I've had good reports of them, but I need to talk to them. We have to make money in this business—we can't afford to take on complete unknowns unless they're really good.'

'What about Rupert?'

'Rupert's got a lot of potential. He'll go a long way, as long as he doesn't allow himself to get side-tracked.'

Once that would have been a critical reference to her engagement—this time the sting in the tail was missing. She was surprised. It must be because he had other things on his mind. Louisa seemed to be his constant preoccupation. He didn't even appear to be giving Bronwen much of a thought, but it was possible she was still in Germany. Her own resentment over his treatment of her—and Bronwen, though she knew nothing of it—at the dance was still smouldering, but it was buried now under more immediate concerns. The way in which she was forced to co-operate with him over Louisa almost created the illusion at times that the three of them were a family, and it was an illusion she couldn't afford to foster. She actually had to remind herself several times a day that he was engaged to another woman.

Once he had disappeared into his study, she took the opportunity to put a few more stitches into the curtain while she waited for Louisa to reappear. She became absorbed, and then realised as a car drew up in the drive that Louisa was taking a very long time over her hiding-place.

Two young men got out of the car. Alex was showing them into his study when she emerged from the library, and she was struck by their deferential manner. It told her suddenly how much that tycoon image had changed for her. His struggles with Louisa had shed a new light on him. She grinned to herself. She had no doubt he would win in the end, but it was good for him to meet with a bit of opposition from time to time! Apart from herself and his daughter, she felt sure that no one else had the nerve to take him on.

A quick tour of the bedrooms, long gallery and attics failed to discover Louisa. There was a chance she might have got side-tracked into spending time with Ellen, and, trying to suppress a nagging little fear about the tunnel, she headed for the kitchens, checking the downstairs rooms on the way.

'Where's the entrance to the tunnel, Ellen?'

The housekeeper looked at her in surprise. 'Funny you should ask that—Louisa's been on about it all morning, Miss Sophie! She asked me to take her down to show her the cellars. That must have been about twenty minutes ago... I turned on all the lights for her, but I had to leave her down there—I had cake in the oven.'

A glance at the shelf where the heavy-duty torch was kept revealed that Louisa must have borrowed it.

'I'd swear it was there this morning,' Ellen said. 'The little monkey!'

A cold hand clutched at Sophie's heart. Trying not to think of what might have happened—and Alex's reaction once he found out—she followed Ellen, who had taken a second torch from a drawer, to lead the way down to the cellars.

The lights, still switched on, revealed a series of connected rooms, neatly stacked with a variety of objects for storage. There were piles of logs in one, and old items of furniture in another, but no sign of Louisa. There was no electric light in the furthest room, and the dark shapes of old brewery barrels loomed along one side. The rest of the cellar appeared to be empty, while opposite them was a dark rectangle—a doorway.

Ellen shone the torch on it. 'That's it,' she said. 'There's a bit of a passage first, and then a door that opens into the old tunnel. I don't think it's locked, only pushed to. Don't go in—hadn't we better find Mr Alex?'

Sophie shook her head. 'He's got a business meeting. Besides, she may not be down here at all.'

'I'll hold you personally responsible'...

Her first hope was that Louisa would have been too frightened to go any distance into the passage. Where Ellen shone the torch through the dark rectangle she saw the door-frame more than twenty feet away, and the open door at the start of the tunnel itself. Then the tunnel curved away into the darkness. Something white lay on its floor—an old sack? It didn't look much like one. With a sinking feeling in the pit of her stomach, she knew she would have to go that far at least.

'I don't think you should go in there alone!' Ellen cautioned again. 'I'm going back for Mr Alex!'

But the thought of Alex's anger—so much for her courageous opposition to him!—and a vision of Louisa, alone and frightened and trapped somewhere down there, spurred her to her next decision.

'Don't worry, Ellen.' She sounded far more confident than she felt. 'I'm only going in a little way. Anyway, I'm sure Louisa hasn't gone in here—not on her own.'

She took the torch from Ellen's hand, and nervously entered the connecting passage. It smelt musty and dank, and she hoped fervently that as much as she had to explore would be structurally sound.

But as soon as she passed the doorway to the tunnel the floor became uneven, rising and dipping unpredictably, and she noticed too that the walls, which curved away to her right, were in an increasingly poor state of repair, long cracks opening up the brickwork. At several points the roof had been propped up with extra timbering, once or twice almost in mid-passage.

The white thing looked less and less like a sack the nearer she approached it, and with a start of dismay she recognised the sweater Louisa had worn that afternoon, draped round her shoulders. Her heart quickened with fear—Louisa *had* been into the tunnel! It was possible she had dropped it accidentally on her way back to the cellars, frightened at last by her own daring, but, if so, where was she now?

She tried calling, shining her torch into what seemed the endless darkness. 'Louisa! It's OK, it's Sophie—I'm coming to find you!' The sound of her voice seemed to fall dead.

The torch-beam petered out in utter blackness. The air was stale, and she could imagine how people suffocated in underground tunnels. Then she found that the impenetrable darkness ahead was a roof fall, blocking the passageway completely. A new fear clutched at her—could it have fallen in the last twenty minutes, since Louisa had been down there? She tried to gather her wits. Surely the air would be full of dust? She would *have* to find Alex.

She tried shouting again. If Louisa were safe on the other side of it, she would be able to answer. Silence. The only sound was the blood pulsing in her own ears. If the fall was very dense, it might baffle the sound of her voice, or if Louisa was hurt—unconscious—she wouldn't be able to hear her...

Hating the darkness behind her, and the thought that she might be leaving an unconscious child, she started to make her way back. As she rounded the curve, she saw the rectangle of light, bright and welcoming, at the end of the passage. Then a man's figure filled the bright frame.

'*Sophie*—come out of there! Where the hell's Louisa?'

It was Alex. He sounded furious, and she quailed at the thought of the imminent encounter. He must have seen the beam of her torch approaching him in the darkness, and he was coming down the passage towards her.

'Ellen says she's been down the tunnel—I thought you were supposed to be looking after her!' He was at the doorway now.

'I'll hold you personally responsible'...

'It's not my fault!' she shouted at him, her voice high and nervous. 'She *knew* she wasn't supposed to——' But she never finished the sentence. Her attention on Alex, she was no longer taking care where she put her feet, and at that moment she tripped. Thrusting out her hand automatically towards the wall to save herself, she dropped the heavy torch, and, in trying to keep her balance in the inadequate light, she stumbled against one of the wooden roof props that had been leaning at an awkward angle. What followed seemed to happen in awful slow motion—the timber fell forward ahead of her, and another beam it had propped across the ceiling crashed diagonally into the passage. As it did so, the entire roof collapsed in front of her.

She heard Alex shout again, 'Sophie!' a terrible urgency in his voice, and then, as in a nightmare, there was choking dust as old mortar followed the stones, and an avalanche of earth—or that was what it sounded like. Instinctively, she had jumped back as the first prop had gone, but with the fall of the stones she had been plunged in darkness. The torch was buried irretrievably beneath the huge pile that cut her off from the cellars.

For the first few seconds after the fall had ceased, she was paralysed.

Then a wave of sheer terror engulfed her—she was buried alive! She was trapped between two roof falls in utter darkness and she would suffocate once the air ran out! And Alex—had he been underneath the roof when it collapsed?

She felt a scream rising in her throat, and her heart was thumping wildly.

'*Sophie*!' At the sound of the familiar voice, a wave of thankfulness flooded through her. He was all right— he would know what to do! He always knew what to do; that was one of the galling, infuriating, wonderful things about him. She could forgive him anything now, if only he got her out! She tried to steady her breathing. Panicking wouldn't help. Then she heard her name again.

'*Sophie*!' There was that note of urgency in it, with something else she didn't stop to analyse.

She could have cried with relief. 'I can hear you, Alex!' She shouted as loud as she could—she heard him well enough, but an irrational fear took hold of her that by some mysterious law of physics her voice would be trapped in the tunnel with her.

There was a pause, then, 'Are you all right?' He sounded perfectly calm now, in control.

'No—yes! Get me out!'

'Louisa isn't with you?'

'No.' She wouldn't tell him about the sweater until later. It wasn't a problem she could usefully discuss through a mound of earth, and there was nothing he could do about it anyway until he reached her.

'Keep back from the roof fall,' he warned. 'There might be more to come down!'

She protested at once, trying to keep the fear out of her voice, 'I can't see—it's pitch-black in here!'

This time there was a thread of amusement through his obvious relief. 'If you can find the strength to argue, there can't be much wrong with you! But keep back— I might need Sam's help. I'll have to send Ellen to find him...'

Silence.

She sneezed. 'Alex?'

'What?'

'I just wanted to make sure you were there!' she said foolishly.

There were dull scraping and thumping sounds after that, and several times she heard him cough. It was a curiously reassuring sound. She felt behind her for the wall. Her hand met the cold, damp stone. She edged backwards towards it carefully—if the roof directly above her collapsed, in the darkness she would be completely helpless. Cautiously, she sat down. The passage floor was the cold of stone under her. She could hear constant shovelling sounds, but it was impossible to tell how fast time was passing. She wrapped her arms round her knees. She still had Louisa's sweater; it was far too small for her, but she draped it round her shoulders.

Louisa—where was she? Somehow she felt convinced that she wasn't in the tunnel. She'd never have left her sweater lying there like that—it was too chilly. She *must* have dropped it on the way out.

She heard Alex sneeze.

'Sophie...?'

'Yes?'

'Just making sure you're still alive! There's never a dull moment with you, is there?'

She laughed. 'It's pretty boring in here right now!'

A feeling of intense longing for him swept through her—if only he got her out of here, it would all be different! She would have to accept the fact that they would never be lovers—but they might at least be friends. It couldn't satisfy her, but it would be better than nothing. Lovers... Of course.

It was all so simple, and it had been staring her in the face all along. What an idiot she had been not to see it! But she had been so busy hating him, and resenting him, and trying to get revenge on him, that falling in love with him had got confused by everything else! She was in love with him—she had no doubts whatsoever about that now—but the knowledge came to her with a sense of dismay. There could be no surge of joy, no sudden flood of happiness, because there could be no future for her with him. Bronwen was Alex's future, not Sophie Carter. They would have to be...just friends.

She thought she heard voices, and the shovelling noises stopped. Had Sam arrived to help? There was a pause and then she heard Alex's voice again.

'Sophie...? It's all right—Louisa's safe! She was hiding and Ellen found her. I've sent her back up to the kitchen. She won't be looking for any more tunnels in a hurry—she says she never went down here, and she's terrified at what's happened to you!'

She debated the wisdom of telling him about Louisa's jersey, and decided to keep her own counsel. The child was probably in enough trouble already.

When the first ray of light from Alex's side of the earthfall broke through, she knew just what a hibernating animal greeting the spring must feel like, but she still had to wait. He couldn't take the risk, however small, of another fall from the roof, by creating an unsupported tunnel beneath it, and when she finally wriggled her way head first towards that welcome glow of light she found that he'd had to reinforce the excavation with a makeshift framework of old timbers collected from the cellars.

As she emerged with difficulty into the glow of the tunnel, now lit by a couple of hissing spirit lamps, Alex caught hold of her wrists and dragged her clear, Louisa's sweater falling from her shoulders as he did so, to lie in a crumpled heap on the ground. She saw him glance at it as he pulled her to her feet. She swayed unsteadily—and it wasn't until that moment that she realised how very real her own fear of further collapse had been. She hadn't let herself think of it until then.

He held her away from him, his eyes examining her critically.

'You look wonderful...!' he said, his voice suddenly gruff in a way she'd never heard it. 'Only next time you want to do a DIY demolition job, read the book of instructions first, will you? There are some things your *Successful Businesswoman* can't tell you!'

For one brief second she looked at him, dark hair full of dust and a long smear of dirt on one lean cheek, and she thought he looked wonderful too, in a way that was very, very different from the handsome tycoon she'd hated that day in the recording studios...

Then his arms went round her, so tightly that she thought he was going to crush her, and she clung to him as though she'd been drowning, her face buried in his shirt. In the inadequate lighting, she'd been aware that the passage had been heaped with spilled earth and tools, and there was the acrid smell of fallen earth in the air— but for a moment, conscious of Alex's arms like a vice round her ribs, and the tangy spice of aftershave in the collar of his shirt, it seemed like paradise to her. And she was free!

'Oh, Alex!' she choked. 'I'm *so* glad you're here!'

'Of all the bloody stupid...!'

She felt his lips on the side of her face, and then she was aware that he was kissing her in a way he had never kissed her before. Somewhere, it seemed a long time ago, she'd come to the conclusion she should never have let herself get involved with him physically, but now, half in a daze, she held tight to him, responding fully to the urgency and real passion she could sense in him. Then she remembered Bronwen.

Guilt acted like a bucket of cold water thrown over her. She tried to push him away, dragging her mouth from his and turning her face aside. 'Don't—you mustn't!' she protested incoherently.

He didn't answer; he was kissing the side of her face, and the line of her jaw.

'Don't!' she said again, more clearly this time. 'You can't do this to Bronwen!'

He looked down at her, tracing the line of her lips with one dusty finger. 'Do what to Bronwen?'

Her pulse seemed to be racing, and she didn't know whether it was delayed shock, desire, relief or what, but she could hardly think straight. 'Alex, for heaven's sake—you're engaged to her!'

'I'm not. I never was!'

She looked at him, only half believing. 'But you said— at Betty's—"Here's to the second time round"!'

From the sideways smile, she guessed he was deriving considerable private amusement from this. 'Bronwen's second time—not mine.'

He'd known, ever since her attempted 'blackmail', that she had believed him engaged to Bronwen. So why, if it wasn't true, had he let her go on making such a stupid mistake—unless of course he was just enjoying the idea that she was jealous? 'You could have told me before!' she pointed out resentfully.

'Why—what difference would it have made?'

'Well, it . . . I . . .' Then it dawned on her—he'd been waiting to catch her out, of course!

She didn't know how to go on. Despite what he felt for her physically—and she'd just had some evidence of that—he probably didn't care about her at all in any way that really mattered. She was determined to give nothing away. 'Why have you got pictures of her all over the house?' she challenged.

He was stroking her hair. 'Come on, Sophie, that's a bit of an exaggeration! *One* picture in my study. There's a picture of Louisa in there too, and one of Rupert— somewhere. Bronwen's my cousin—more like my sister. She's my age, and we were virtually brought up together.'

It still didn't add up. 'Why was Betty congratulating you, then?'

'She wasn't,' he said firmly. 'She was talking about her nephew. It's taken him years to get round to proposing, and he and Bronwen should have married each other long ago. She's a very quiet person. She likes a quiet life and so does he, but she married a different sort of man the first time round, and it turned out to be a big mistake. They were both unhappy. She's been divorced for a couple of years. Does that answer your question?'

She still wasn't satisfied. 'But why did she go to Germany with you?'

'She didn't. She works for a cosmetics firm—she had business there. We weren't even on the same plane, and she's still there now as far as I know. Anything else?'

She shook her head. There was no Bronwen in his life—no engagement—no reason why... Why *what*, exactly? She had to remind herself yet again that he had never expressed any favourable feelings for her whatsoever.

'Let's get out of here,' he said quietly. 'It's no longer safe.'

And that was true in more ways than one.

She was through the remaining section of the tunnel, which had seemed so long to her when she had set out, in seconds, and the cellar's electric light was dazzling after the lamps. She blinked dazedly as Alex followed her towards the steps.

And there was Ellen, just coming down them—and behind her Louisa, white and frightened. Ellen's face, drawn in worried lines, cleared with relief. 'You're all right—thank goodness! Louisa's been fretting...'

Alex stopped, hands on hips, and faced his daughter. 'I thought I told you not to come down here again!'

'Yes, but Ellen——'

'And I thought *you* told *me* you hadn't been in the tunnel?'

'I did... I——'

'Then how come Sophie found your sweater?'

She shrugged. 'I don't know,' she said in weak defiance. And then burst into tears. 'Daddy—I'm sorry!' She took the bottom steps in a flying leap and ran to him, jumping up into his arms and clinging to him tightly, burying her face in his neck.

'Daddy...the tunnel—I *did* go in! And Sophie's...' She didn't finish, choked by a flood of tears.

Alex carried her towards the cellar steps, cradling her against his chest. 'It's all right, sweetheart. She's fine. Nothing happened to her...' He started up the steps towards the kitchen.

There was something about the father and daughter at that moment that seemed to exclude anyone else. Sophie looked at Ellen, and the housekeeper smiled.

'I reckon she'll be all right now,' she said.

Yes. Louisa would be all right. But what about Sophie Carter? Now she knew about Bronwen, everything had changed—and nothing had changed. She no longer knew what to do.

CHAPTER NINE

IT WAS late evening before Sophie saw Alex again.

Emerging from the cellars, she had felt nothing but a kind of emptiness; all her emotions had been drained out of her. What should she do now? The brief passion that had taken hold of her in Alex's arms, fuelled this time by the knowledge that he had shared it, had gone. She still wanted him—she loved him, needed him—but it wasn't a love or a need that was mutual. In the tunnel, alone in the dark, everything had looked simple to her. She had discovered she was in love with him, and that seemed like an answer to all her difficulties with him. But of course it wasn't. It was only the beginning of new ones.

Aimlessly, she wandered towards the front of the house. Alex and Louisa seemed to have vanished. His car was still parked by the front door, but the guitarists had gone. He must have got rid of them when Ellen had first found him.

A glance at herself in a hall mirror showed her a wild fury out of a Greek myth. Her hair was standing out from her head in long, untidy trails full of dust, and there were smears of dirt on her face. 'You look wonderful!' Alex had said. At the time, she had half believed it was a genuine compliment—even the sarcasm hadn't been in evidence—but just look at her! Getting into the washing-machine, clothes and all, was her only hope of improvement.

She wandered upstairs for a bath, and almost fell asleep in it; she felt utterly exhausted. Her watch told her it was after five. Where on earth were Alex and Louisa?

Fully dressed again, she went downstairs to the small sitting-room to wait for them. She sat down on the sofa, intending to put a few pieces into a jigsaw she and Louisa had started together, but she must have fallen fully asleep, because suddenly it was dusk outside. She found that she was curled up on the sofa, and that someone had put a rug over her. She sat up, dazed, stretching her arms and yawning. She must have slept for hours! Perhaps she should have another look for Alex—and wasn't it about time Louisa was in bed?

It was at that moment the door opened, and Alex himself stood in front of her. She stared at him, arrested in mid-yawn.

When she had last seen him, his hair had been full of dust like hers, and powdered cement had smeared one cheek. Now he had bathed and changed it seemed as though he was back to the man she had been fighting one way and another ever since her arrival at Derrham. She felt a little twinge of disappointment. She couldn't help hoping something might be different.

'So you're awake!' His eyes took her in with one keen glance. 'I thought you might have run off again when we couldn't find you.'

She tried to gather her wits. 'You and Louisa were the ones who ran off!' she countered. 'You disappeared!'

'Only as far as Betty's...' He crossed to the sofa and stood looking down at her. Instantly all her feelings changed gear again. 'You looked exhausted when I came in here earlier—your hands felt like ice. I thought you'd die of hypothermia.'

He'd watched her, touched her, when she was asleep?

'Who put the rug over me?' she asked awkwardly.

'I did. Get your feet off that,' he said. 'You're taking up all the space.'

Before she could argue, he had sat down next to her, one arm stretched along the back of the sofa behind her. It was the first time he had ever done anything like that. She found that she was breathing very unevenly, desperately conscious of his closeness. What did he want?

'What made you think I'd disappeared?' he asked. 'I'd only gone out to the stables. It seems Louisa's been laying plans to get Goofy back, and she thought she'd strike while the iron was hot, and I was in a mood to indulge her. She wanted him there and then—I think she'd set it as a sort of test of my affection for her. I came to look for you, but you'd vanished.'

'I had a bath.'

His eyes appraised her. 'So I see.'

The way he was looking at her made her feel as though every single clean garment she'd put on was completely transparent. It was all she could do not to blush. She didn't offer a comment.

'I left a note for you. Didn't you see it?'

She shook her head, her newly washed blonde hair falling over one shoulder. 'Where?'

'On the hall table. What did Louisa do with the "treasure", by the way?'

Again Sophie shook her head. 'I've no idea. What possessed her to hide herself instead of the trophy?'

Idly he stretched out those lean, tanned fingers and took up the errant strand of hair. 'Wanted a bit more of my attention, I suppose.' There was a curious silence. She felt as though there was something she should be saying—or he should be saying—but she wasn't sure what it was.

'So you've got Goofy back?' she began again. The way he was playing with her hair, absently winding it round his fingers, was getting to her. It was just as though he were caressing her skin.

'He's in one of the loose boxes for the night. I'd resisted fetching him earlier because Betty had lent him to a pony club. I didn't want Louisa to find out in case it upset her, but luckily Betty had arranged to get him back today.'

'Oh,' she said.

She was convinced now that the real conversation was going on on a very different level, one on which she wasn't at all sure of her replies.

'So you hadn't run off again,' he said, after another pause.

'What do you mean?' she asked carefully.

'Wasn't that what you were doing the day I found you on the road in the rain?'

There was no point denying it. He'd already discovered how flimsy her excuse had been when her father had rung.

'Why *did* you run away?' he persisted.

She looked at him sideways. 'You can be very rude sometimes, Alex Tarrant. I'd had enough!'

Those subtle fingers touched her chin, turning her face fully towards him. 'Had enough of what exactly?' he said softly.

His touch was doing incredible things to her; she could hardly trust herself to reply. 'You want a list?'

His eyes, that astonishing navy blue, weighed her up. 'I think it's time we discussed a few things, don't you?'

Something in his voice told her that now, at last, they were having the real conversation. But she was sure she knew what he was going to say, and she didn't want to hear from him right now that, while he didn't share them he knew what her feelings were all about, and how it had to be a casual thing, no strings attached, he didn't love her et cetera, et cetera. She'd heard all that once before, from Tony. Only what had happened with Tony seemed like child's play.

'How would you feel if I asked you to leave?' he said.

Her heart missed a beat. So she hadn't had the least idea what he was going to say! The feeling of finality almost overwhelmed her. It wasn't until that moment that she knew just how desperately and hopelessly she was in love with him, because underneath, hidden even from herself, she had been fostering a pathetic hope that he might return just a little of that love.

Her eyes filled with tears, and she turned her head away quickly to hide them. She'd been such an idiot all along. Why had she let it come to this? She should have left Derrham that very first time Rupert had found her packing. She should never have stayed on to let Alex persuade her into working for him, looking after Louisa, sharing his family life...calling the tune time after time.

She tried to blink the tears away, and shrugged. 'I'll miss Louisa, of course I will——' that was as casual as she could manage '—but I suppose I'll be able to get on with more work. That is if you still want me to do the tapestry?'

'Why should I change my mind about it?'

'I don't know,' she said lamely. 'I just thought that as you want me to go and——'

'Sophie——'

'I won't be doing any more work here for you and——'

'Sophie——'

'What?'

'I said *if*...'

The pressure of his fingers at the side of her jaw forced her to face him again, but she wouldn't meet his eyes.

'You're not going to admit it, are you?' he said gently. 'I've yet to meet anyone so stubborn...'

'Admit what?' she asked bleakly.

'This,' he said.

She looked at him, surprised by something new in his tone, and for a brief instant his eyes blazed down into hers and she was astonished by the desire she thought she could read in them. Then his mouth touched hers. She put her hand up to his face instinctively, and his

skin felt smooth, and newly shaven, and there was still
that familiar tang of expensive aftershave. There was
nothing she could do after that—she was completely
helpless. She realised that in the art of seduction she was
a complete novice; already he was melting her and he
hadn't even begun.

She found herself kissing him back. Her lips parted
willingly under his; all her resistance since the dance
turned into a sweet, eager fire that leapt to meet a flame
that she knew for certain this time was in him.

It was a long time before he released her. His lips persuaded her, and his hands, exploring her body beneath
the loose-fitting shirt she had put on, awoke sensations
in her that were entirely new to her. She found herself
lying underneath him, the unfamiliar weight of his body
on top of hers a new stimulus to desire. Nothing in her
past experience had prepared her for the ache of longing
she now felt for him. It was as though in this explosive
release of the tension that had been building up between
them for so long they had blown open the doors to a
furnace. Far from satisfying, the contact had stoked up
new fires. If he had wanted to take her there and then
on the sofa, he would not have found one shred of resistance in her.

At last he broke off, to look down at her, his eyes so
dark that they were nearly black.

'Sophie . . .'

She gazed up at him in silence. She couldn't even
speak.

'Are you sure you want this . . . ?'

She nodded, and reached up to draw his head down
to her again.

She seemed to have been waiting all her life for this
moment, but Alex was in no hurry. He began to kiss the
side of her face, and then her throat, while his hand
traced her lines of her body. She was drowning in a sea

of senses, every part of her achingly alive to his touch...

It was he who first heard the car. Sophie was aware of nothing but the insistent demands of her own body. When he broke off what he was doing, she tried to draw him back to her, but he caught her hands in one of his and held them.

Then, faintly, they heard the doorbell. They lay for a moment in a dazed stillness. The summons was repeated.

Alex gave a reluctant groan, and rolled himself off her, to sit on the edge of the sofa. 'That has to be Rupert—he's forgotten his key.' His voice sounded rough, a way she had never heard it before.

She pushed herself up, only half aware of reality, but somehow the spell had been broken. All she was conscious of was that she had been about to give herself to him...and it had been the very worst idea she had ever had in her life!

'I'll let him in!' she said, wondering if her words made sense. She felt as though she had just been dragged back from another world.

'Don't get up...'

But a sort of panic took hold of her now. She *had* to get up—she had to break the spell completely! They would have made love, but how much 'love' would there have been in it? Hers, and hers alone. She had to know that Alex felt more for her than just desire before she could take such a risk.

'No—I'll go!' she insisted, with a sudden desperation. She didn't wait to let her resolution slacken, but swung her legs off the sofa, smoothing her rumpled hair. She didn't even wait to adjust her clothes, but began to pull down her skirt as she made her way to the door. She tried to make a joke of it. 'You can't go,' she said. 'You haven't got a single shirt button done up!' And vanished into the passage.

She made her way unsteadily into the hall, and towards the inner door, but as she did so she heard the front door open—it hadn't been locked. Why hadn't Rupert bothered to try it first?

Footsteps approached the hall. Then the inner door opened, and as she stepped forward to greet him she stopped dead in her tracks...

She had come face to face with her living self.

She couldn't believe it... Her first reaction was that she must be looking in a mirror. Perhaps Alex had left one there—he had just bought it; he had forgotten to mention it. No explanation, no matter how far-fetched, seemed weirder than the truth: that she was facing a woman who looked *exactly* like herself! For what seemed like a lifetime, she stared in frozen recognition, the shock paralysing her where she stood. Never would she have believed that another human being could have looked so like her. And then, suddenly, a whole lot of things fell into place.

She began to notice the little differences—the trace of lines about eyes and neck, the brighter, harder line of the mouth, that expensive gold of a tan that wasn't the product of an English sun. The way she herself might look in ten years' time? She hoped not. With a horrible cold certainty, she knew who this was, though she couldn't stop herself asking for confirmation.

'Who—who are you?' The words seemed to stick in her throat.

The answering voice was deeper, harsher than she'd expected. 'Vicky Tarrant. And who the hell are you?'

She didn't reply. What could she say? A name alone was no answer. To have been told this woman was Vicky Tarrant would have meant nothing to her only a couple of months ago—there was more, so much more, information needed to answer that question.

She had that information now—and boy, did she have it—with a vengeance! Every atom of desire Alex had generated had disintegrated.

When she could make that uncanny mistake about herself, who wouldn't take her for Vicky? Because that was *exactly* what Alex had done. It all seemed to make sense now... Everything, even from his first hostile reaction to her, attracted to her as the woman he both loved and hated, and still couldn't do without. He had seen her as Vicky. Then he had tested her, and she had imagined he was looking for signs that would prove to him she was a very different character from his ex-wife. But he had been looking for similarities, not differences, and he had found enough to make her an adequate stand-in for the woman he really wanted. If they had gone to bed, she would have been Vicky for him, and she couldn't have borne it. She had never had a lover. To have given herself to the man she cared about so much when he didn't love her would be unendurable.

If she stayed now, it would amount to a tacit acceptance of her role as a Vicky substitute. And she would always be at the mercy of that potent sexual attraction—the pattern of their relationship had shown it again and again, and while he could use it she would inevitably dance to his tune. No matter how he behaved towards her, he had only to touch her and she would melt like wax in a flame.

She knew exactly what she would do; the plan was ready, waiting in her head.

When she heard Alex come out into the hall, she was halfway up the stairs. He must have come to find her and Rupert. Then she heard him say 'Vicky!' very low, and Vicky's answer. The tone of it didn't surprise her. It fitted in with everything she had heard about Alex's ex-wife.

'Missing me so much you had to find a look-alike, Alex?'

She didn't wait for his reply.

It took only a few minutes to pack. This time she checked every surface—no forgotten train tickets or purses. There were two sets of car keys on a table in the library. She wouldn't attempt to drive the Porsche—she would probably set the alarm off and he would hear it. She scribbled a note on the back of an envelope she found in her handbag, and left it where the Jaguar keys had been lying. He would discover it in the morning. He had gone upstairs with Vicky to Louisa's room.

She let herself silently out of a side-door. The Yale catch would lock itself behind her. The car was parked on the gravel in front of the house. Louisa's room overlooked the lawns at the back; it was unlikely Alex would hear the purr of the engine or the sound of the tyres on the drive from there.

It was the kind of summer darkness that wasn't really dark. It would be light very early. She didn't want to think about Alex, or what had happened, and her ability to keep going depended on that. Just at the moment she felt as though there was enough adrenalin in her to take her all the way to London, or anywhere, in fact, so long as it was miles and miles from Derrham—and the man with whom she had fallen so disastrously in love.

She had planned to leave the car in the station car park at Hereford, and the keys at the ticket office once it was open. She glanced at the clock on the dashboard—it would be a long wait for that first train. The petrol gauge caught her eye; the needle was close to the 'empty tank' mark—no question of going to London, and now even Hereford might be too far. She would go to Leominster instead. She could park the car there undisturbed and have a sleep until the first train was due. It was a better idea anyway. Alex would go to Hereford to look for the car once he'd found her note, and by the time he'd been there and guessed what had happened, she'd be on her way home. She found that she could make perfectly normal, rational decisions about it all, just as though the pain in her throat was the prelude to a cough or a cold, and not the ache of unshed tears.

When a sharp bend in the road came up very suddenly, she realised she was driving too fast. She braked abruptly, causing the car to skid with a squeal of tyres—lucky that at that time of night there was so little traffic on the country roads! But it gave her a bad fright, and she pulled into the next field gateway to calm down. She didn't know how long she sat there.

Why had she ever thought she could play with fire and not get burned—and how had she imagined it would all end? That safe, comfortable image of her ideal man had faded now beyond retrieval. What had replaced it was vital, challenging and totally destructive. Her ideal man would have married her. But Alex... No, Alex wouldn't have married her. He would have made her his mistress, so that she would be there when he wanted Vicky. He had no interest in the person called Sophie. It had taken that last extraordinary meeting to make her see what had been so plainly obvious to everyone; she should feel ashamed—she had let herself be won over by him with scarcely a struggle. But at the moment, all she could feel was hurt. Very, very hurt.

Eventually she restarted the engine, and finished the journey at almost a crawl. Unsure of the route, she had to stop to read the signposts at every junction, but even so she took wrong turns and went several miles out of her way. The time wasted didn't matter—she didn't like the idea of spending the hours alone in a parked car beside the empty station buildings—but the low fuel level was a worry. She felt very alone. It would have been wiser to wait until morning before leaving. But then she would have risked another meeting with Alex.

She was continually distracted by thoughts of Derrham: the beautiful house, the estate, and the people who worked on it. In other circumstances, it would have been the life of her dreams. And Louisa. She had grown very fond of her, and the fondness was now mutual. She would miss her. Then there was the restoration work; there would be no finishing that now, of course. The tapestry would continue to moulder away, unless Alex found someone else for it. She wondered if he would offer to pay her for the work she'd already done; the curtain was almost finished. In a sudden burst of resentment, she was determined that if he did pay her she would take every penny. It was her job, after all. She'd earned it.

It was so late that it could be called early by the time she reached Leominster. She had opened the car window to keep herself alert, and through it she heard a first bird as she turned into the station forecourt. She drew up right in front of the station buildings, where the car would be easiest to find, and turned off the engine. The darkness had the hint of the grey of a summer dawn, but it would be some hours before there was a train she could catch, and there wasn't enough petrol to go back to Derrham now even if she'd wanted to.

Was there a train timetable posted up? She couldn't remember. Automatically, she closed the window and got out of the car, locking the door and putting the key in her pocket.

'*Sophie*.'

Her heart gave a lurch. It was a voice she could never mistake.

Very slowly, with a feeling that was only half reluctance, she turned round.

CHAPTER TEN

THE Porsche was parked by the overgrown bushes at the edge of the forecourt—she had driven straight past it without even noticing. The driver's door was open, and Alex was striding towards her.

The sight of his tall figure, dark hair slightly ruffled as though he had just run a hand through it, made her heart stop. She didn't want to see him—he couldn't have any good reason for coming to find her—not any reason she would like to hear, anyway.

'Alex!' Her mouth was dry. 'What are you doing here?'

'I might ask the same—what the hell are you doing here?'

It was the first question he had ever asked her, and suddenly she was back in that pub with Rupert, when Alex had first seen her—but, instead of the anger in his voice, this time there was only weariness, and an overwhelming relief. It wasn't what she had expected. His eyes, that familiar intense blue, seemed to burn into her.

She didn't know how to answer. In the end, when the silence had lengthened unbearably, she said, 'I'm going home.'

'Why?' he asked bluntly.

A milk van rattled past in the street beyond the station parking area. There was no one else about.

'I—I thought it was time to leave.'

'At eleven o'clock at night, in my car?'

'You said I could borrow a car if I wanted one!' Habit made her defensive. 'I left a note for you—I wasn't taking it for a joy-ride!'

174

The flicker in his eyes told her he recognised that reference. 'I know. I found the note. You've been hours getting here.'

He had been waiting for her. He must have known about the petrol and guessed she wouldn't go to Hereford. She shivered, but it was only partly with cold.

He was looking at her closely.

'Where are the keys?' he asked.

Automatically she handed them to him. He unlocked the driver's door.

'Get in.'

She obeyed. She didn't have the strength left to argue. He walked round to the passenger door and opened it. 'It's not much use locking one door when the other's open!'

He sounded amused, and his mouth quirked in that characteristic way as he got in beside her, but she looked down at her hands in her lap. He turned towards her, one elbow propped on the back of the seat, and she was aware of his scrutiny.

'Just answer me one question, Sophie—*why* did you leave?'

She couldn't answer. She wasn't sure she could face all that about being like Vicky—he would probably deny it anyway.

'There's nothing to discuss,' she said hopelessly.

'I think there is.' There was another long pause, while he studied her thoughtfully. And then with no warning, no introduction, he said, 'Tonight, before Vicky turned up, I was going to ask you to marry me.'

At first she thought she couldn't have heard him correctly. She turned to him. He was still watching her, a question in his eyes.

She licked her dry lips. 'What?'

'Will you marry me?'

Marry...? She *had* heard him; he had said it twice now. Typical of Alex—several moves ahead so that you couldn't see what sort of game he was playing. That was one of the things that had antagonised her in the past, and one of the things, paradoxically, she admired in him. But it didn't change anything. He couldn't have the real Vicky—so he was going to make sure of the substitute.

'No,' she said.

She thought she saw the twitch of a muscle in his cheek, but she couldn't be sure—there wasn't quite enough light. And his expression hadn't changed. 'Why not?'

She might as well say it; for the first time in her stormy relationship with him, she hadn't the energy to put up any more defences. 'I won't be a second Vicky,' she said, with finality.

This time she saw clearly the surprise on his face in the lift of dark eyebrows. 'What on earth makes you think I'm looking for one?'

She was the one who had brought up the subject, and there was no getting out of it now. She stared again at her hands in her lap, and a lock of hair fell forward over one cheek, partly hiding her face.

'You don't...really want *me*, Alex,' she began awkwardly. 'I didn't understand anything until I saw her and just how alike we look. Then everything fell into place— the odd reaction I kept getting from people...your reaction when we first met...the way you've treated me since then. You're attracted to me only because I look so like her. Sometimes you even acted as though you hated me—for not being her, I suppose!' She couldn't sense any reaction in him at that. She had expected one, but he waited for her to continue. She went on rather desperately, 'You're always so sarcastic—so dismissive of what I do and ready to blame me for anything that goes wrong! You're just using me, Alex—you've said you want to marry me, but you haven't said one single word about *loving* me! Is it so surprising the answer's no?' All her objections seemed to have spilled out at once.

His next words were very quiet. 'You don't make it easy for either of us, Sophie, do you? If I told you I loved you now, I suppose you wouldn't believe me.'

Her voice felt choked. She had to swallow hard. 'No, I wouldn't.'

'Then I'm not sure how I'm going to convince you.' Perversely, at that moment, she found herself desperately wanting him to persuade her—but it had to be the truth.

'I don't know how you've reached this conclusion that I want another version of my first wife,' he said slowly, 'but I can only tell you that you're wrong—completely and utterly wrong! Even Rupert must have told you we didn't have a successful marriage.'

'That doesn't mean to say you're not still attracted to her.' She glanced at him sideways, but the grey darkness still hid the subtle changes that might have hinted at his deeper reactions. 'Rupert told me at the very beginning that you had me keyed into your mental computer as somebody different. I didn't understand at the time, but he meant Vicky—all the antagonism was for her. And,' she finished bitterly, 'all the attraction!'

'I admit I had you wrong to begin with,' he said carefully. 'You did look so like her at first that I thought you must be almost her twin, in character as well, not just looks. You gave me quite a shock that day Rupert introduced you in the bar. I was sure you were Vicky sitting next to him. When you turned round, for a moment I could have been back ten years.'

'I suppose after that I did go along with the image you seemed to have of me,' she agreed reluctantly.

'You put on a very good act that first time, but you couldn't have kept it up.' His tone was surprisingly gentle. 'You are your own person, Sophie, different in every way.'

Different. So perhaps he hadn't been looking for similarities after all...

'How am I so different from her?' she persisted. She had to know it all, if there was going to be a future. She didn't dare let herself hope.

He was silent for a moment, and then he stretched out and brushed a strand of her hair aside, tucking it behind her ear. It was impossible to remain unaffected by his touch; inside she was melting already, and she had a struggle to appear indifferent to it.

'When I married Vicky,' he began slowly, 'I was too young to appreciate that the packaging doesn't always give you a clue as to what's inside the present. Look at Vicky now and you can see very clearly what she is— hard as nails. It was always there, in the line of her mouth, and in her eyes, but I didn't know how to read it.' He paused, and then went on, 'What you're telling me is that I've fallen for the same packaging all over again, but you're not giving me the credit for having learned anything in ten years! It's not a question of legs and eyes and hair, Sophie. It's what's underneath the skin... That's the turn-on—and just as quickly a turn-off, believe me.'

He was silent again, and then he said, 'Vicky and I married too young, and we grew apart instead of together; we had different ideas about what mattered, different tastes, different interests. In the end we made each other extremely unhappy.'

'So how am *I* different?' she persisted. 'How do you know *I* won't be another Vicky in ten years' time?'

She didn't look at him, but she could hear the smile in his voice. 'My sweet, naïve Sophie, Vicky was a calculating little madam from the day she was born, and you don't even know the meaning of the word!'

'I do!' she insisted, turning to him suddenly in protest. 'I calculate all the time—about my life, where the next penny's coming from...'

That made him laugh outright. 'Darling, you act on pure impulse! The kind of calculation I'm talking about has nothing to do with working out whether you can pay the rent!' He stretched out a finger, and she felt it slide down her cheek in a caress—like the one he'd given her so unexpectedly before he'd left for London with Rupert. 'You give the impression sometimes of being very sophisticated——'

'*Me*?' He couldn't really believe that!

'Yes, you! When you dress up and stalk along on your high heels, you look very aloof and woman-of-the-world...' And then his next words cut her down to size! 'But you're a lot younger in some ways than you'd like to appear, Sophie Carter!'

'What do you mean?' she demanded, stung into a reaction. He probably knew just where her insecurities lay, but she'd better hear the worst—his picture of her wasn't the one she might have expected.

'What about jumping to the conclusion that a man's a lustful and callous seducer just because he kisses you in a way you've obviously never been kissed before?'

'I didn't!' Typical. He'd hit one rather uncomfortable nail right on the head at the first attempt. He laughed, and she knew her denial had merely confirmed him in his opinion.

'All right, then,' she began again, piqued, 'why else am I different?'

He was silent for a moment, and his reply had a new, more serious tone. 'Because you love Derrham for what it is. You fit in here—you only have to ask Ellen and Sam about that. Vicky hated the Welsh borders; unlike you, she couldn't see any romance in them. For her Derrham was a status symbol, not a family home, and she considered its contents as disposable assets.'

'Was it you who divorced her, then?' She was pondering Ellen's comment about infidelity.

'No—we came to an agreement. We were making each other too miserable. But there was a lot of resentment. She felt bitter about Derrham; I felt bitter that she took Louisa when she hadn't wanted her in the first place.'

'What do you mean?'

'She didn't want children. I did,' he said simply. 'She made it clear after she'd had Louisa that she wanted her own life. The man she thought she'd married was a businessman with a glamorous lifestyle, but she resented Derrham's claims on my interest and time and she started to spend more and more time away.'

'Were there—other men?' she asked hesitantly.

'Yes.' The brevity of his reply dismissed any further questions along that line. She sensed the old wounds that must lie beneath what he had just told her, but from his even, almost indifferent tone she guessed that they must have long since healed over.

'Where's Vicky now?' If she was still at Derrham, there would be no going back.

'*En route* for the States. She only turned up to ask if I'd look after Louisa—indefinitely, it seems. She's getting married again, and her future husband isn't keen on the idea of a child—he's already got a grown-up family.'

'So Louisa's been dumped?'

'In effect—yes. But that's not the way it's got to look. She thinks she's here on a long holiday.'

Suddenly she was stabbed by conscience—she hadn't given Louisa a thought since Alex had got out of the other car! What had he done with her? She turned to him abruptly, her eyes wide with alarm. 'Where is Louisa? If Vicky's already on her way to the airport, you haven't left her all on her own?'

'You don't have much of an opinion of me as a father, do you?' He sounded amused. Perhaps he had left her with Ellen.

'Oh,' she said, rather abashed. And then added quickly, 'I think you're probably a wonderful father, given half a chance! It's obvious you adore her!'

That made him laugh again, and his thumb touched her chin as he forced her to meet his eyes. 'Talking of adoring...' he said. 'I never thought I'd want to marry again—and I never imagined that the person to change my mind would be someone like you...!'

'So you do care about me, then?'

His voice was still amused, but it had that deep note that got to her on a very special level. 'Yes, Sophie! I do care about you—though I don't think "care about" is what you're asking! I was hoping that after the dance there might be time to show you exactly what I felt about you, but you were so defensive. And then all the problems of Louisa blew up.'

'Of course I was defensive!' she exclaimed. 'You'd just pulled a very mean trick on me!'

He laughed, and she saw his eyes glitter in the grey light. 'Without Bronwen I might never have known just how strong your feelings about me were! Incidentally, Bronwen thinks we'll be very happy together...'

The lightest pressure of his fingers against the side of her face told her what he was going to do, and she gave herself up completely to the gentlest of kisses. When he broke off, she looked across at him.

'Afraid you might scare me away?' she asked softly. 'That wasn't quite your usual style.'

He smiled, and drew a line across her lips with one forefinger. 'You haven't agreed to marry me yet! And I'm never completely sure where I am with you. I think that's one of the intriguing things that surprised me into falling in love with you!'

'"Never a dull moment",' she quoted. 'You haven't actually told me what you've done with Louisa.'

'Ah,' he said. 'Rupert's back.'

She was instantly suspicious. 'Did he know Vicky was coming?'

That amused him. 'No! And he missed her by about twenty minutes—just in time to solve my problem about coming to look for you. I thought it was time he put in some practice as a responsible uncle. Now, are you coming back to Derrham with me?'

There was a long silence while she weighed up everything that implied. Then she met his eyes. 'I suppose I am,' she said.

They drove home in his Porsche—he would arrange to have the other car collected later in the day, when the garages would be open and there would be no difficulty getting petrol.

'By the way,' he remarked casually, as they were threading the maze of lanes in which she had lost herself so effectively only an hour or so earlier, 'on the subject of your favourite book, I've got a few suggestions to make to the successful businesswoman—if you're still interested in going on with the tapestry restoration business. That is, of course, always assuming you're going to marry me. The only answer you've given so far is no, but I was hoping I might have changed your mind about that. Have I?'

She didn't need to think about it any more—it was one of those clear-cut cases when all the facts had been assembled beforehand, and for once there was no mistaken conclusion to leap to.

She felt suddenly insanely happy. And very tired. 'You're a hard man to resist, Alex Tarrant, and I don't think I'll ever win where you're concerned!' Her regretful sigh rapidly became a yawn. 'I suppose you have...'

He stopped the car at the gates of Derrham. There was the long drive and the dip, and the billowing trees and the little rise, just as she had seen them only a few weeks ago with Rupert, and there was the castle with the first faint colour of the early morning sun on its walls.

'You're sure you're prepared to cope with all this?' he asked, turning to look at her.

'All what?' She'd been in a wonderful daydream.

'Taking on Louisa, and Derrham, as well as the difficult bastard you seem to think I am.'

'I don't think that!' she protested feebly.

His eyes flashed that amazing deep blue. 'Yes, you do! When you're not within a couple of inches of giving yourself to me, you like to keep me at barge-pole's length! You really don't trust me those last few inches, do you?'

She could feel a blush creeping up her neck, and it wasn't nearly dark enough to hide it. 'You mentioned Derrham—and Louisa?' she prompted, side-tracking. He had weighed her up, summed her up, and seen through her with that keen glance of his! It was astonishing that he still wanted to marry her, given all the things he must now know of her!

Mercifully, he took the hint. 'It won't be easy—Louisa's been very messed about. She feels she's been betrayed twice, first by me and now by her mother. She's been carted round for the last five years while Vicky has gone from one man to the next, and she doesn't even remember how many people have looked after her. She's very fond of you, but that doesn't mean she'll leap at the idea of a stepmother...' Louisa's stepmother... She couldn't yet take that in.

'And Derrham takes up half my life, Sophie. The estate is something that's been left to me, in trust for the future. For Louisa, and for any other children we might have.'

That seemed even less real—that the clever, impatient, successful Alex, the man she had once thought had everything, the man many women must have wanted, would one day be the father of her own children! Any minute she would wake up, and find that she'd fallen asleep at the station, and the train was coming in that would take her away from him forever...

'I think you ought to know,' she said carefully, with a sideways glance at him, 'that if I marry you I'll want enough children to fill up Oliver Cromwell's table. If the prospect daunts you, you'd better drive me straight back to the station!'

'You realise that table seats twenty, don't you?' he asked.

'Yes!' she said brightly. 'Well...no, I didn't... I hadn't added up...'

'I'll give you a calculator for Christmas. And perhaps I ought to point out that producing eighteen children—seventeen if you're counting Louisa in—takes some time.' He was looking at her, a new light in his eyes.

'Is that an indecent proposal, or has it put you off marrying me for good?'

'There's nothing indecent about it,' he said softly. 'Hold out your hand.'

He took something out of his pocket, and suddenly it flashed green in the light—green as the grass in the fields of Derrham.

The emerald was set in heavy gold; it was old, and very beautiful. She gasped. 'Is this for me?' That meant...he must have been pretty certain all along of being able to persuade her back to Derrham!

'It's the Tarrant family ring. You *are* going to marry me, aren't you?'

Unfortunately, she couldn't think of one single further objection. 'Oh—yes. Yes, I am!'

That made him laugh again, as he slipped it on her finger.

'Didn't... Wasn't...?' She didn't know how to ask.

He read her unspoken question. 'No. It still belonged to my mother when Vicky and I were engaged. It was only a couple of years ago that she gave it to me—an unsubtle hint that I might consider marrying again.'

Her old doubts about the Tarrants and the Strettons gave one dying twitch. Alex was a long way from being the feudal snob she had first thought him, but what about the rest of his family?

'What's she going to think of me?' she asked, very insecure all of a sudden.

He sat back, his arms folded, considering her. There was a look in his eyes she'd never seen before, but this time she had no difficulty in reading it.

'You know what to do with your knife and fork?'

'So it *was* a test, then—that first night you told Ellen to put the silver out!' she accused.

'Nothing of the sort. I wouldn't be so inhospitable.'

'You didn't want me to marry Rupert,' she pointed out. 'You were hoping I'd lick the soup plate!' Then she thought of something. 'What do you think Rupert's going to say about this? You know I'm engaged to him!'

'Rubbish!' he said shortly. 'I never believed that for a minute.'

'I think you did—at first! You were horrified!'

'Let's say... I was only ninety-nine per cent appalled.'

They entered the house very quietly. She began to yawn.

'I don't suppose...' It was an unexpectedly careful beginning for Alex. 'I don't suppose I could persuade you to go to sleep in my bed?'

She opened her eyes. 'No,' she said firmly. 'You could not!'

'Or to let me sleep in yours?'

'It's marriage or nothing, Alex Tarrant! As you pointed out earlier, I don't trust you at all those last few inches!'

He groaned. 'And I suppose you want a proper wedding?'

'As proper as the circumstances require,' she said primly. 'Whatever that means.'

His reply was thoughtful. 'I'm not sure I can wait that long...'

'This is a very big bed,' she said, stretching languorously. Her bare toe touched Alex's. An arm slid under her back, and all of a sudden she found the whole length of her naked body against the length of his.

'To get back to this question of a brother for Louisa...' he said softly.

She turned, so that she was half lying on him, one arm across his chest. 'Or a sister?'

'No. She's definite about it,' he said firmly. 'A brother—with your hair and my eyes. As soon as possible. Hadn't we better make sure of it?'

She gave him her sideways look. 'What do you think we've been doing for the last few hours? It's just as well we persuaded Rupert he and Louisa might like to take up Betty's suggestion, and carry on the party over at her house!'

Absently he traced a line down her nose, and across her lips. 'Your father was enjoying himself. He's got a good sense of humour!'

She laughed. 'He needed it—even Rupert thought three days was rather short notice! It's a pity you couldn't wait for your mother to get back....'

'I waited those three whole days,' he pointed out. There was a meaningful pause.

'You know,' she said, ignoring the fingers that were travelling slowly and seductively down her spine, 'I'd quite like to meet your mother.'

'I think my mother would "quite like" to meet you...Mrs Tarrant!'

MILLS & BOON

HEARTS OF FIRE by Miranda Lee

Welcome to our compelling family saga set in the glamorous world of opal dealing in Australia. Laden with dark secrets, forbidden desires and scandalous discoveries, **Hearts of Fire** unfolds over a series of 6 books, but each book also features a passionate romance with a happy ending and can be read independently.

Book 1: SEDUCTION & SACRIFICE
Published: April 1994   *FREE* with Book 2

Lenore had loved Zachary Marsden secretly for years. Loyal, handsome and protective, Zachary was the perfect husband. Only Zachary would never leave his wife…would he?

Book 2: DESIRE & DECEPTION
Published: April 1994   Price £2.50

Jade had a name for Kyle Armstrong: *Mr Cool*. He was the new marketing manager at Whitmore Opals—the job *she* coveted. However, the more she tried to hate this usurper, the more she found him attractive…

Book 3: PASSION & THE PAST
Published: May 1994   Price £2.50

Melanie was intensely attracted to Royce Grantham—which shocked her! She'd been so sure after the tragic end of her marriage that she would never feel for any man again. How strong was her resolve not to repeat past mistakes?

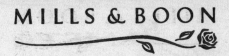

MILLS & BOON

HEARTS OF FIRE by Miranda Lee

Book 4: FANTASIES & THE FUTURE
Published: June 1994   Price £2.50

The man who came to mow the lawns was more stunning than any of Ava's fantasies, though she realised that Vincent Morelli thought she was just another rich, lonely housewife looking for excitement! But, Ava knew that her narrow, boring existence was gone forever…

Book 5: SCANDALS & SECRETS
Published: July 1994   Price £2.50

Celeste Campbell had lived on her hatred of Byron Whitmore for twenty years. Revenge was sweet…until news reached her that Byron was considering remarriage. Suddenly she found she could no longer deny all those long-buried feelings for him…

Book 6: MARRIAGE & MIRACLES
Published: August 1994   Price £2.50

Gemma's relationship with Nathan was in tatters, but her love for him remained intact—she was going to win him back! Gemma knew that Nathan's terrible past had turned his heart to stone, and she was asking for a miracle. But it was possible that one could happen, wasn't it?

Don't miss all six books!

HEART ⟨TO⟩ HEART

Win a year's supply of Romances
ABSOLUTELY FREE?

Yes, you can win one whole year's supply of Mills & Boon Romances. It's easy! Find a path through the maze, starting at the top left square and finishing at the bottom right.
The symbols must follow the sequence above.
You can move up, down, left, right and diagonally.

Please turn over for entry details

HEART ⟨T⟩⟨⟩ HEART

SEND YOUR ENTRY NOW!

The first five correct entries picked out of the bag
after the closing date will each win one year's supply
of Mills & Boon Romances (six books every month for
twelve months - worth over £85).
What could be easier?

Don't forget to enter your
name and address in the
space below then put this
page in an envelope and
post it today (you don't
need a stamp).
Competition closes
31st November 1994.

**HEART TO HEART Competition
FREEPOST
P.O. Box 236
Croydon
Surrey CR9 9EL**

Are you a Reader Service subscriber?   Yes ☐   No ☐

Ms/Mrs/Miss/Mr _____ COMHH

Address _____

_____

_____

_____ Postcode _____

Signature _____

One application per household. Offer valid only in U.K. and
Eire. You may be mailed with offers from other reputable
companies as a result of this application. Please tick
box if you would prefer not to receive such offers.   ☐